MEN BEHAVING BADLY

ALSO BY TIM O'LEARY

Nonfiction

Warriors, Workers, Whiners & Weasels

Fiction

Dick Cheney Shot Me in the Face, And Other Tales of Men in Pain

The Corona Verses

MEN BEHAVING BADLY

STORIES

BY

TIM O'LEARY

RARE BIRD
LOS ANGELES, CALIF.

This is a Genuine Rare Bird Book

Rare Bird Books
6044 North Figueroa Street
Los Angeles, California 90042
rarebirdbooks.com

FIRST PAPERBACK EDITION 2025

For more information, address:
Rare Bird Books Subsidiary Rights Department
6044 North Figueroa Street
Los Angeles, California 90042

Set in Minion
Printed in the United States

10 9 8 7 6 5 4 3 2 1

Library of Congress data available upon request.

CONTENTS

ACKNOWLEDGMENTS

MY THANKS TO JEFF, Kym, David, Marti, Darrell, and Maureen, for their continued support, inspiration, and sometimes brutal, soul-crushing literary criticism drunkenly delivered during some of my favorite evenings. My advice, as always: Write good prose. Drink great wine.

Literary journals, magazines, and anthologies are the lifeblood of short story writers, and my appreciation to the following publications for supporting the stories in this book:

"Made Men" was originally published in *Ellery Queen Mystery Magazine.*

"Annemarie (Hillbilly Love Story)" was originally published in *What We Talk About.*

"The 100-Year-Old-Sheriff" was originally published in *Grievous Bodily Harm.*

"A Very Brady Funeral" was originally published in *Into the Void.*

"Secret Creek" was originally published in *The River in Us All.*

"Reunion" was originally published *in Aestas.*

"The Impersonator" was originally published in *We've Been Trumped.*

My friends and family realize I have a penchant for naming characters after them, and I want to assure everyone that just because I christened a criminal, pedophile, drug dealer, or other heinous individual with your moniker, it doesn't mean I love you any less. In literature, there are just more creeps than heroes.

Finally, thanks as always to Moshe Shulman and my beautiful wife, Michelle Cardinal.

MADE MEN

CATTERLY NEVER PICTURED HIMSELF going out this way, standing in some godforsaken heat sink, clad in the official old man's uniform of big-butt cargo shorts and a Tommy Bahama Hawaiian shirt, guzzling white wine—*probably Pinot Grigio, for Christ's sake*—and surrounded by a bunch of other wrinkled codgers, an entire community playing footsie with the gravedigger.

No, his retirement was supposed to be a pleasant extension of the first seventy years of his life. A payoff for decades of waking at 3:00 a.m. to rush to the barn, where he'd shove his arm elbow-deep into a bovine's poontang to extricate her slimy calf. A bonus for the bones he'd shattered while herding all manner of belligerent beasts. Recompense for the mutilations he'd accumulated while stringing fence and clearing brush, including the four-inch violet scar tattooed across his left thigh, a painful memento of the Husqvarna chainsaw that bucked in 1984. He'd had to duct-tape his leg to keep from bleeding to death before making the forty-minute drive to the Bozeman hospital, the seat of his F-150 permanently stained bloody. *Jesus, he missed that truck.*

He'd worked his ass off making his spread damn near perfect and intended to enjoy it until they celebrated his passing by dumping his ashes into Shy Creek. He wanted to transform into a gentleman rancher—like Ben Cartwright on *Bonanza*—and let some other buckaroos do the hard lifting. Amble the lowlands with a twenty-gauge crooked under one arm, his black lab Belle whimpering at the scent of pheasants. Drive into Livingston once a week to hoist a few at the Murray Bar with Eric and Dave while laughing at the citidiots in Resistols buying overpriced Western art in the galleries. Fling a fly into the Boulder River when the hoppers were thick. That all sounded like a fine way to spend your golden years.

But Pearl put a quick end to that fantasy. "We can't stay here in the winter," she'd announced. "Too cold. I'm done driving any vehicle that needs snow tires, and I'm too feeble to pick your old bones off the porch when you slip on black ice and break your hip."

Of course, Catterly knew that wasn't true. His wife might be pint-sized, but she was far from feeble and had the temperament of a mama grizzly. If push came to shove, she'd find a way to get his ass to a doctor. But the decision had been made, and that was that. Pearl law. Case closed.

So here they were in Oro Valley, Arizona, relocated to a stucco cracker box with a bunch of other AARP members equally terrified of a little precipitation. Vista View, marketing speak for: a neighborhood of old farts living in identical huts in the middle of the desert. Their little house came with a golf cart, and a long list of rules. Catterly decided that retired folks must be aspiring Mussolini's, spending their final breaths' developing new regulations: No parking on the street after 7:00 p.m. Garbage cans must be removed from the curb by eleven. Visitors are required to display a pass in their windshield or prepare to be towed.

Why'd people get so damn ornery as they aged?

When he'd replaced his old rusty mailbox with a beautiful new aluminum number, the first correspondence he'd received was from the architectural committee. "Your mailbox does not conform to neighborhood guidelines. Please consult section D, paragraph L of your resident's manual, and replace it with one of the three authorized models. You have thirty days before a fine will be levied."

Jesus, were they living in Arizona or 1939 Berlin?

Old Mrs. Weekly, the chairman of that group of knotheads, would drive by every morning in her bright blue Cushman to remind him what a sinner he was. "Don't forget, you need to replace that mailbox," she'd warn, wagging a finger while he walked Belle.

"Yeah, yeah, I heard you," he'd mutter, and defiantly flip the bird once she was out of sight. He missed the freedom of five thousand acres, with his nearest neighbor a thirty-minute drive away.

But her condemnation was nothing compared to the brouhaha he'd created with the "rattlesnake incident," as it came to be known. Catterly had spent a lifetime interacting with dangerous creatures, developing a particular aversion to serpents. He'd read there were thirteen different species of rattlers in Arizona, and the triangle-headed bastards loved to slink around the neighborhood in search of a little shade. Maybe cozy up in a window box, or lounge on the welcome mat. He'd been working in his driveway, vacuuming the Taurus, when he saw a big western diamondback slither into the garage. He grabbed a shovel and scooted the snake out the door and onto the front lawn (or what passed for a lawn, as there was no grass, only gravel, pursuant to regulation 193). The snake decided to stand and fight, curling into a battle position and striking with dripping fangs. Catterly jumped back, yelled a few strong expletives, and cleaved the tool down hard, extricating the rattler's head from its body. Eyeing the thick tail of rattles, he looked forward to popping them off, adding to his forty-year collection stored in a cigar box back on the ranch. But first, he didn't want the damn thing to bleed all over his perfect white pebbles—which was probably a violation of some statute—so he picked up the beheaded serpent and was heading toward the backyard to bag or bury it when he heard the gasps. There was Mrs. Weekly, with what appeared to be most of the ruling elite of Vista View hanging out her golf cart, pointing in horror.

"Oh, my God," she screamed. "You killed that poor animal."

Catterly was confused. Slaying rattlesnakes was a public service where he was from. "It's a rattler," he said, thrusting the corpse toward them. "Damn near bit me." Reptile gore drizzled down his arm.

"You can't murder the wildlife," a boney drink-of-water by the name of Alfred Upman piped up. "This is their home too. It's against the rules. You should have called animal control."

"I sure as hell am not waiting around for animal control, and neither would the snake," Catterly hollered, as the rattler spasmed in his hand in the throes of some post-mortem death dance, oozing more blood and coagulum, and eliciting horrified moans from the crowd. Two more golf carts pulled up, entertainment of this caliber rare in Vista View.

The next day his illegal mailbox was the repository of hate mail from the Homeowner's Association and a few offended residents of the PETA persuasion. He was warned that he was in violation of section C, paragraph B, and the killing of wildlife would not be tolerated. Catterly contemplated gathering up a big bag of rattlesnakes and dumping them on the committees' gravel lawns to see how they'd react.

But he swallowed his anger and decided to grin and bear it, intent on doing a little penance to please his wife. Pearl had never enjoyed ranch life like he did. Sure, she'd had a love affair with a few of the horses—and who could resist a pink Montana sunset—but he knew the isolation had gotten to her. She was a social type, loved gossiping with her girlfriends, enjoyed dinner parties and seeing the latest movie. Back home, Thursday had been her favorite day of the week. She'd head into Livingston to have lunch with the gals, then spend the afternoon volunteering at the library. Now she loved Vista View as much as he detested it, and Catterly figured that given the forty-five years she'd dedicated to him, it seemed the least he could do to spend four months a year living in a place that made her happy.

"We just need to get out so you can make a few friends. Take advantage of all the good stuff this place has to offer," Pearl said.

So here they were, sipping white-goddamn-wine on the deck of the community center after enduring an afternoon concert by Mr. Pat Boone. The entire affair posed three big questions in Catterly's mind:

1. Who goes to a concert at 3:00 p.m.?
2. Didn't Pat Boone die twenty years ago, and if so, who was the tight-skinned old man singing "Moody River"?
3. If they had to listen to an elderly performer, why not Willie Nelson?

But Pearl was enjoying herself, happily surrounded by her new book club near the pool, so he slipped off to explore the bar and find a real drink. Scotch in hand, he watched a group at the card table play Gin. He'd spent a fair amount of time with the game while stationed in Vietnam and played in a monthly soirée at the Elks Club in Livingston, so he was pleased to find an endeavor he might enjoy.

After about five minutes, one of the players, Joe Whitworth, rose and threw his hands up. "Sorry, gentlemen, I'm done. Hey, Rattler," he smiled, thrilled to have an opportunity to kid Catterly with his new nickname. "Care to take my seat? Be careful; these guys are *real* snakes."

Catterly forced a smile, shook a few familiar hands, and took Joe's chair. There was an alpha dog he didn't recognize who'd clearly been winning, and he rose again to introduce himself. The man looked out-of-place, doughy fat, wearing a rumpled linen suit jacket. His hair and mustache were dyed dark burgundy, an unnatural shade that could only be created with strong chemicals. Color-corrected tresses or obvious cosmetic surgeries were a serious faux pas in Vista View, where signs of aging were a badge of honor. The man stayed seated and tentatively offered a chubby paw with a look Catterly read as disdain. His handshake, limp and rubbery, was delivered palm down, as if he were European royalty.

The player to his right, whom Catterly knew only as Stan, did the introductions. "Catterly, meet Thomas DeVito. Thomas, Catterly is a great guy to have around if any rattlesnakes show up," he laughed.

"Nice to meet you, Tom," Catterly said.

"Thomas, not Tom," DeVito said curtly. "Or Mr. DeVito. We play for twenty-five cents a point. Are you in?"

Mr. DeVito? What was this guy's problem?

Catterly tried to place the accent. Eastern: Boston or New York, with an Italian lilt. Made sense; the guy was dressed like a Sicilian immigrant circa 1952. He did some quick math. With four players, that put the potential stakes at somewhere around fifteen or twenty bucks a game, not bad for an old folk's home. "Sounds great," he answered.

DeVito dealt the first hand, which ended extraordinarily fast when he knocked for four on the first round. Catterly and all the players had high counts, and a collective moan emanated from the table.

"Thomas, you're a hell of a player," Stan said, in a sycophantic tone.

As the winner, DeVito held the deal and quickly gathered up the cards. The second hand went three rounds, but this time DeVito ginned, taking a huge lead. Catterly realized he would be way off in his calculations if the guy kept winning like this.

On the third hand, he watched the deal a little more carefully. DeVito's plump fingers were fast, but Catterly was sure he palmed three aces, moving them to the bottom of the deck and into his hand. Given the dismal eyesight and trusting nature of the other players, nobody seemed to notice. When it was Catterly's turn to draw, he pulled an ace, flipped to show it to DeVito, and said, "Care to make a side bet you have the other three in your hand?"

"You'll soon find out," he said brusquely.

DeVito won the hand—with three aces—which put him over 100 and ended the game. Since DeVito had been keeping score, he consulted a pad, and said, "That puts me at 109, and nobody else scored, so you each owe, let's see, $27.25."

"102," Catterly said.

"What," DeVito gave him a sharp look.

"Your score was 102, not 109. I was keeping track," he said. "Not a big deal. An easy math error, but we each owe $25.50."

DeVito snarled his bottom lip and pushed the pad forward. "It's 109, as you can see right here. Unless you're accusing me of cheating."

"No, not accusing you of anything, except being really lucky where aces are concerned and maybe not very good at math." Catterly reached into his wallet and took out a twenty, a five, and a dollar, as he stood from the table. "But I'll split the difference with you, or at least get close. Here's $26.00. Keep the change." He threw the money at DeVito.

"You owe $27.25," DeVito barked. "You some kind of welcher?" The other players stared at Catterly open-mouthed. "Where I'm from, we have a way of dealing with deadbeats that you might not like."

"Doesn't sound like you live in a very friendly place," Catterly said, "but this is Arizona, and $26.00 is all you get. It's a damn sight more than you deserve." Sizing up the fat man, Catterly contemplated that he might be about to get in his first fight in over forty-five years, which was titillating. He figured he'd easily put DeVito down, and a little danger would be a welcome distraction at this point in his life. Then he considered the impact a physical confrontation would have with the Homeowner's Association. There was undoubtedly something in the guidelines about old men rumbling. If "Rattler" progressed from killing wildlife to pummeling other residents, they might consider him unhinged, and the blue hairs wouldn't stand for it. While he'd personally love the opportunity to get ejected from Vista View, he couldn't do that to Pearl. He reached into his pocket and counted out another $1.25 in quarters, nickels, and dimes. "All right, if another buck and a quarter is that important to you, here you go," he said, pouring the coins on the table. "Use it to buy some better hair dye. Gentlemen," he turned to the other players, "not only are this guy's math skills awful, but when he deals, he likes to palm low cards from the bottom of the deck, so I'd be careful."

DeVito pushed back the table to stand up. "You insult me and accuse me of cheating? You just made a big, big mistake." He thrust a finger.

Catterly fought back the strong urge to laugh. DeVito was even less impressive standing than he was hidden behind a table. Probably five-foot-six, as wide as he was tall, he resembled a Super Mario Brother. "Hush up. You're embarrassing yourself. If you really need to cheat, practice a bit," Catterly said as he turned to walk away. "And I wasn't kidding about the hair dye. Try Grecian Formula. It looks good in the ads."

"Screw you," DeVito yelled, spittle flying. "You're going to regret that."

Catterly felt it best to move on and headed toward the opposite end of the bar to order another cocktail, the adrenaline rush providing a pleasant buzz. Pearl spotted him through the open door and, unaware of his situation, gave a happy wave. A few minutes later, Joe Whitworth sidled in next to him and ordered a gin and tonic.

"Well, you like to live dangerously, don't you?"

"Meaning what?" Catterly replied.

"You do know who you just offended?" Whitworth dropped his voice.

Catterly motioned at the card game, which had resumed. "You mean Luigi Mario over there?"

"Jesus," Whitworth said. "I guess you don't know who Thomas DeVito is. You made a big mistake, and I suggest you go apologize. DeVito's Mafioso. A Made Man. He was a big shot in the Genovese crime family. Some kind of enforcer. Word is, he's killed a dozen men or more. I heard he likes to beat guys to death with a baseball bat."

"A Made Man? You've been watching too many De Niro movies," Catterly said. "Him, a killer? The only thing he'll kill is himself with high cholesterol."

Another man pushed in next to them. Catterly thought his name was Brian or Bill. "Did you tell him who DeVito is?" he asked Whitworth.

"I did, and he doesn't care," Joe answered.

"Well, then you're out of your mind. You don't want him coming after you. You'll end up in a shallow grave somewhere in the desert. I heard he beat a guy to death with a tire iron."

"Tire irons, baseball bats..." Catterly smiled. "What happened to the good old days when you used a gun or knife to kill somebody?"

"Quit joking around. I tell you, he's the real deal," Whitworth said. "If I were you, I'd make amends."

Catterly glanced at DeVito, and the two made eye contact. DeVito scowled, raised a hand formed into the shape of a pistol, and cocked his thumb as if firing. Catterly smiled, held out his hand as if accepting an air kiss, brought two fingers to his lips, smacked the tips, and flung a hand at DeVito, leaving a middle finger raised.

"Jesus," Joe said, shaking his head. "I'm telling you, that's not a guy you should screw with."

"Yeah," Catterly laughed. "I'll probably end up with a bloody horse head in my bed." Slapping his forehead as if he'd forgotten something, he added, "Wait a minute, there's a rule against that, isn't there? Section B, paragraph L. No decapitated animals allowed in the bedroom."

Whitworth and Brian or Bill frowned, opting to move away in search of a safer space.

Two weeks later, Catterly and Pearl were back at the community center, this time to celebrate a birthday. Terry Walton was Pearl's new BFF, inspiring her to act with a girlish delight Catterly had not seen since the Reagan administration. Pearl had transformed from a churlish country gal into the belle of the ball. She kept her busy social schedule on a new iPhone 13 that she also used to FaceTime with their granddaughter, despite the fact she had once decried any mobile technology as "time-wasting horseshit." Every afternoon she was off to meet with another group: bridge or book club, Vista View Film Lovers, and several other organizations seemingly based on drinking vino in the afternoon. Catterly had to admit, as much as he hated Vista View, he was enjoying the impact it had on his wife.

Their sex life, which had suffered the same doldrums as most couples who'd been married over forty years, had undergone a resurgence, beginning when the book club had read *Fifty Shades of Grey.*

Catterly worked hard to find his own desert delights and had discovered a couple activities that made the area more bearable. He honed his shotgun skills at The Second Amendment Gun Club, shooting trap twice a week. He'd also discovered his own delightful afternoon libation. There was a tavern within golf cart range that specialized in daiquiris, a drink he would have never considered in Montana but which now seemed somehow appropriate. He understood why Hemingway reportedly downed fifteen per day but limited himself to a couple per visit.

As the group celebrated the birthday girl with more wine, Catterly excused himself to the bar to order his favorite frozen cocktail. He was immersed in the typical Vista View chatter—funerals, sports, and grandkids—with the ever-present Joe Whitworth, when Thomas DeVito walked in, flanked by two wrinkled flunkies.

"Ah, snake man," he said with disgust. "I haven't forgotten you. Don't think you'll get away with insulting me. I have a long memory, and your time is coming."

"Hey, DeVito, how are you?" Catterly said brightly. "I was thinking about you. I saw an old movie last night: *Throw Momma From the Train.* It starred that little guy, Danny DeVito, and I realized you're probably related. Maybe he's your younger brother? Shame he got all the looks in the family. And the height," Catterly added.

DeVito's fat face flushed red. "You're a dead man. Dead. You won't know when or where, but it's coming," he said as he strutted off.

"Did I mention how nice your hair looks?" Catterly yelled after him. "What do you call that color? Rusty magenta?"

"You know that one of these days, there'll be a knock at your door, and some big goombah will cart you off to the forest and shove you into a woodchipper," Whitworth said.

"Nonsense," Catterly answered, ordering another daiquiri. "There's no forest around here."

ONCE A MONTH, CATTERLY made the pilgrimage to Tucson, a voyage he complained about to Pearl but secretly enjoyed. The stated goal was to visit big box stores and stock up on low-priced cleaning and paper products and bags of frozen shrimp from Trader Joe's, but to Catterly it was his musical road trip. He'd plug his phone into the jack in the Taurus and crank up the volume to sing along with the Bee Gees, Donna Summer, Gloria Gaynor, and the other disco stars he'd never admit he enjoyed. Even Pearl didn't know *Saturday Night Fever* was his favorite album, a secret passion he'd acquired in 1977 when they saw the film on a date night in Bozeman. Catterly had been lobbying for *Smokey and the Bandit*, but Pearl won a coin toss and, given her Travolta fixation, made the obvious pick. Catterly complained before and after the movie but had been secretly affected by the music, and on his next trip to town, bought the soundtrack on cassette tape, nervously assuring the clerk it "was a gift for his daughter." Expressing anything but complete disdain for that kind of music would have ruined his reputation in Montana, so he kept his growing collection of disco tapes in a locked box in the barn, only bringing them out when he had a long, solitary drive.

Technology had transformed his musical stash into a secret playlist dubbed SNF on his iPhone, which made him nervous whenever Pearl grabbed it to make a call. Seeing his discomfort, she sometimes kidded him. "What's the problem? You been texting a girlfriend or watching a little porn?" Catterly mused how odd it was he'd rather be suspected of infidelity or perversion than admit he enjoyed the high-pitched genius of the Brothers Gibb.

During the drive, he'd feel fifty years peel off his old frame, swaying in his seat and singing along. Even though he knew it could have serious legal consequences, a tiny cooler sat on the passenger seat, loaded with two cans of Budweiser: one for the trip to the store, and one for the return. He loved to sip slowly as he drove, the feel of a cold can between his thighs providing a nostalgic pang. While he could have found closer places to shop, he picked this destination for its long, straight drive.

Flannigan's Classic Cars was on an acre near the main shopping district, and Catterly stopped on every trip. Flannigan specialized in old muscle cars from the sixties and seventies, the lot packed with bright Trans Ams, Chevelles, Mustangs, and other glossy American iron. On the ranch, it was impractical to own any vehicle that couldn't withstand the indignity of rock chips, broken shocks, and cracked windshields, and aside from the many beloved pickups he'd destroyed on rutted fields and washboard roads, Catterly never had affection for an automobile. But Arizona would be nirvana for a classic ride, and he was working up the courage to become a buyer. Cattle prices had been strong last year, so money wasn't a problem. He knew Pearl would accuse him of another mid-life crisis, or perhaps now an "old-age" variation, but the fantasy of tearing down a desert highway on a steamy night with 400 HP roaring out loud headers haunted him.

He wandered the lot, running his palms down smooth hoods, until he saw it: a 1965 Pontiac GTO convertible, midnight gloss blue, with a white interior and top. This was the car. He stared at it as if seeing an old lover for the first time in decades. A salesman, recognizing tell-tale buyer signs, rushed to open the vehicle. Catterly leaned back in the wide bucket seat, wrapping a paw around the Hurst shifter, imagining running through the gears in bright moonlight, wind whipping what was left of his gray locks.

Forty-one thousand dollars. Well past his budget, but perhaps they'd take less. What would Pearl say? Would it make him look like a foolish old man intent on reliving his youth, like the codgers he saw tooling around in Corvettes?

Catterly shook his head, told the disappointed salesman he'd give it some thought, and returned to his Taurus, suddenly feeling the weight of seven decades. The very idea of spending so much money on a childish purchase suddenly seemed ridiculous.

Shell-shocked, his next stop was Costco, a nine-block drive from Flannigan's. Though there were two Costco's closer to Vista View, he preferred coming to this one. Grabbing a roller bed cart, he entered the store from the east, intent on exploring every aisle. He loved the surprise, the adventure of discovering huge quantities of stuff he absolutely didn't need, and sometimes didn't know existed, at 30 percent off MSRP. A month earlier, he'd purchased a thirty-six pack of LED lightbulbs, overjoyed with the purchase until Pearl pointed out they only had twenty light fixtures in the entire house, and since the bulbs lasted seven years, he'd be almost ninety before they used them all up.

Hungry, he worked his way toward the food section, intent on grazing at the many tasting kiosks. It was there that he spotted DeVito. Initially, he didn't recognize him without his rumpled suit. His Italian nemesis was working at the Captain Nemo Seafood kiosk, handing-out fish sticks in tiny paper cups.

"Line caught and really delicious." He smiled at a passing couple. He was clad in a pirate's hat, ruffled shirt, and buccaneer pants, which made him appear even more dwarf-like. Catterly stayed out of view and moved behind DeVito. "Tender haddock. Healthy for kids," he said to a family pushing a baby cart. Catterly noticed he no longer spoke with the East Coast accent, instead projecting a Midwestern, grandfatherly voice.

Moving into DeVito's sight, Catterly said, "Ahoy, Tommy Boy. Looks like that mafia thing didn't work out. Decided to become a pirate instead?"

DeVito went pale. "Catterly. I'm just..." He searched for an explanation but couldn't find words.

Catterly picked up a packet of the fish sticks, inspected the label, and threw it on his cart. "These look great. I'll take them over to the community center tomorrow. Have the kitchen heat them up, and we can serve them at the Gin game. You should wear your outfit," he said, motioning at the hat. "It makes you look younger. Like you just kissed Peter Pan." He smiled and started to push the cart down an aisle.

"Catterly, wait," DeVito yelled after him. "Can we talk?"

Catterly stopped.

"Finish shopping, and I'll close up here. There's a Starbucks next door. Meet me there in thirty minutes. I'll buy you a coffee." DeVito looked desperate. "Please."

Catterly nodded. "Okay, thirty minutes. But promise me you'll wear the hat. It makes you look taller."

DeVito was waiting when Catterly entered the Starbucks. "I got you a large latte," he said, motioning at a seat. "That okay?" He'd changed into chinos and a white shirt.

"Perfect," Catterly answered. "I can't help but notice you don't sound at all like the Italian guy I met at Vista View. Where are you really from?"

DeVito looked embarrassed. "Denver."

"Denver? Are you even Italian?"

"Nope," he answered. "Jewish. My name's not DeVito, it's Greenburg. The Tom part is real. Tom Greenburg."

Catterly laughed. "Jesus. Why the tough guy act?"

"I don't know," he said, shaking his head. "It just happened. My wife and I bought the house at Vista View to retire. Three months before we were supposed to move in, she got sick. Cancer. She was dead in a few weeks. We'd already sold our place in Denver, so I moved here by myself. I was grieving. Pissed off. We'd planned for thirty years to retire here, and when it was all about to happen, she dies. We'd lost our son in Iraq a couple years earlier, and there was nobody else. Nobody that gave a shit about me, anyway." Tom leaned back in his chair and stared at his cup.

Catterly could tell this wasn't an act. "Sorry about your boy." He didn't know what else to say.

Tom gave him a nod and continued. "At first, I just stayed in the house, didn't go out. Then one night, I was watching *Goodfellas* on TV. I always liked Joe Pesci in that movie. Maybe because he's short too. There are not many short, tough guys. Don't know if you remember, but his name was Tommy DeVito. People never pick up on that. Anyway, I just decided it would be fun to reinvent myself in a place where nobody knew me. Become my own version of Tommy DeVito. I started going to the center, playing cards, building up the story. It was weird, but people were anxious to believe me. Everyone seemed to get a kick out of it. A couple times, I even had a guy who works with me at Captain Nemo's show up and act like he was visiting from New York. He's a big, scary looking dude, and we pretended he was a hit man. Never said it, but people assumed. It made me feel special, but it made them feel good too. Like they knew somebody important. We all want to be associated with someone important. Seemed like a win-win for everyone."

"Jesus," Catterly said. "You went to a lot of trouble. Making up an entirely new identity. Must have been tough to stay in character."

Greenburg was wringing his hands. "I've never achieved much. I worked as a controller at a car dealership. Got by, but not much of a living. Always had trouble making friends. My kid was dead. My best friend was my wife, and suddenly she's gone. Look at me," he said in disgust. "All my life, guys harassed me for being short and fat. But suddenly, I'm a Made Man. Someone to be feared. Important. It felt good. Never experienced that before. I mean, what's wrong with feeling good about yourself? When you get old, people just want you to sit back in your chair and look out the window; forget about your dreams. Just be quiet and wait to die. I wanted to experience something new. Feel important for once. Be a Made Man."

"And this?" Catterly motioned out the window at Costco. "The fish stick thing. Why?"

"Why do you think?" Greenburg answered. "I need the money. Janice's medical bills ate up any savings. Luckily, I'd put a good down payment on Vista View, but I need to work to keep up. I make a few bucks playing Gin. I spend my weekends in Costco and Sam's Club pretending to be a pirate and talking people into buying processed fish parts." He looked around and lowered his voice. "Whatever you do, don't eat those goddamn things. I think they're cured in formaldehyde. Anyway, it's just more pretending. I've gotten pretty good at that."

"Don't you worry about getting caught?" Catterly asked. "You're on display in a busy store."

"I just stay away from Oro Valley. There's plenty of Costcos between here and there. Old people hate to drive. They never come all the way to Tucson. Except for you. Just my luck." He looked at Catterly. "Listen, I know I've been an asshole, and you don't owe me a thing. But do you think we could keep this between us? If it got out, I'd have to move, which I can't afford. I'd be humiliated. Forced to start over. Not sure I could do that."

Catterly sipped his coffee and considered the situation. It occurred to him that Vista View was more interesting with Thomas DeVito in the bar as opposed to Tom Greenburg. Nobody needed another boring retired guy in their life, but a Mafia hit man—that woke everyone up. And a friendly association with a faux mobster might offer certain advantages. Perhaps the nosy biddies would cut Catterly some slack if they feared being dumped in the desert. And Tom was right. Were you supposed to give up on your dreams just because you had a few wrinkles?

"Promise to quit cheating?" he asked Tom.

Greenburg gave him a shocked look. "I wasn't…" He stopped when Catterly shook his head. "Uh, yeah. No more cheating. I promise"

NINETY MINUTES LATER, THE two men were whooping loudly, Catterly piloting the Pontiac GTO at ninety miles per hour down the freeway, as Greenburg's short arms thrust up to catch the gust screaming over the windshield. At Catterly's suggestion, Tom was wearing the pirate hat, which he'd strapped under his chin to keep from losing in the wind. They'd stopped to buy another six-pack, and with a can wedged between his legs, Catterly felt his balls shrink from the delightful chill.

Tom had been a big help with the negotiations. After working at a car dealership, he knew all the tricks, negotiating the GTO down to $35,000. Catterly knew there'd be hell to pay when Pearl discovered he'd traded in the Taurus, but he figured he'd swapped his truck for the golf cart, so it seemed fair. And here they were, Catterly and his new friend, two Made Men, barreling down an Arizona highway, *Disco Inferno* blasting out the speakers, both thinking how wonderful it was to be young and alive.

RAGING

VINCE WAS PITCHED AGAINST a light pole, texting an errant employee, when Danny emerged from the doorway across the street. The sight of his son, happily jostling with a pack of ten-year-olds, transformed his anxiety to joy.

But that was short-lived. As Vince took a step toward Danny, his phone barked the distinctive tone of a rager alert. The screen went red with a message in white block letters. RAGER REPORTED IN YOUR VICINITY. Vince had received many rager alerts, activated whenever a rager was reported in a twelve-block radius. In most cases, it was a mistake, or the rager had already been neutralized, but his adrenaline still spiked.

Danny spotted Vince and waved. Raising a hand, Vince scanned the area for any sign of trouble. He spotted him across the street, a block away, but approaching at a fast clip. A rager, with the sloped forehead and black eyes of a dangerous man, wildly waving his arms and cursing out anything within earshot. Tall and slim, he was clad in a calf-length raincoat covering a dark suit—far better dressed than the typical rager. But there'd been little correlation between appearance and violence; raging was no longer confined to the politically motivated, PTSD sufferers, or addled street people. The disease was mainstream, hitting fast and random and intensifying the carnage, since the affluent had better access to weapons and crowded areas.

The man who'd gone on a stabbing rampage in Pioneer Square was a partner at a major law firm, and according to all reports, he'd been completely normal hours before the episode. The shooter at

Costco was a tech executive who'd gone to the store to buy a new Samsung television but somehow ended up killing three people. Profiling a rager had become as useless as attempting to spot a potential flu victim.

At the corner, the rager kicked a vending machine and then screamed at a hotel bellman, who retreated behind the door. He slammed an arm against the storefront of the Nordstrom's outlet, shuddering the massive pane of glass. A bull-necked security guard protected by a Kevlar vest popped out of the Rite Aid across the street, his fist cradling a holstered stun gun.

Vince had seen this before. A preview of an explosion, and he began to calculate a defensive path while hitting the speed dial on his phone, sending an emergency text to a rager response team, though he assumed they were already on their way. Unfortunately, an attack typically lasted seconds, not the minutes usually required for help to arrive.

Reaching under his leather jacket, he pulled the PROTEC from the holster on the back of his belt. It had become the go-to defensive weapon after gun control measures were enacted to stop the onslaught of mass shootings by ragers. He was encouraged that the man didn't seem to be carrying a weapon. Raging impacted everyone differently. Sometimes it was a short-term affliction manifested by a few hours of crazy behavior but no real violence. In others, it flipped a switch, and they became rabid animals. If the man crossed the street and made any kind of threatening gesture, Vince would douse him with the pepper spray contained in his PROTEC. The PROTEC's oval handle contained the spray, and if that didn't stop the assailant, he would pull the PROTEC's trigger for a more lethal option. With the touch of a button, a rubber and metal sack released, creating a high-tech nunchuck that could extend several feet. The pepper would blind the man, and, if necessary, Vince was confident he could then put the rager down with one or two hard slaps.

Ash Street had been closed to automobile traffic after a rager in a car veered off the road into pedestrians. The city had converted most of the downtown thoroughfares into pedestrian walkways, with concrete blockades at each end to stop traffic. Cameras topped every building, and two rotated as the rager hopped off the curb toward two men, his fake punches punctuated with a barrage of obscenities. The AI software on the cameras was constantly searching for rager-like behavior, and Vince assumed that between his text and the cameras, help would arrive any second. The men held their arms up and retreated. The shouting drew Danny and his friends' attention, and the boys pulled closer together. When Danny looked at his father, Vince motioned at the door they'd just exited.

"Danny, you and your friends go back inside," he said, stepping off the curb between the boys and the man. They hesitated, and then moved toward the entrance, stopping outside. *Of course, they want to see what's going to happen*, Vince thought. *What boy wouldn't? But if the shit hits the fan, they'll get through that door, and short of a police station, there's probably no safer place to be."*

For the last three months, Danny had been taking self-defense classes at Park Dojo. WALK WITH CONFIDENCE, the sign advertised. It devastated Vince to remember that at his son's age, he was heading to soccer practice, not learning the finer points of crushing a man's windpipe. But the group sports Vince enjoyed as a kid were rare, a field full of children posing too tempting a target. Vince lamented that his boy would never witness a professional team playing in a stadium or experience a concert with twenty-thousand shrieking fans. Even going to a restaurant, navigating a maze of scanners and guards, had become an expensive and stressful ordeal.

The rager kept moving and was sixty feet away when Vince revealed his weapon. He prayed the man wasn't too far gone and would hesitate at the sight of the PROTEC. He glanced at the Rite Aid security guard, hoping for assistance, but the man remained glued in front of the store, staring dumbly.

He heard the laughter before he saw the two girls. They'd exited the store to his left, both so immersed in something on their phones that they didn't notice the rager. But the rager saw *them* and, sniffing fresh prey, veered in their direction.

Later, Vince would try to describe the bellow. "He howled," he explained to friends, "like an animal attacking prey. Unlike any sound I've ever heard a human make."

The rager broke into a sprint. *He's going to rip them apart*, Vince thought, moving to intersect as he pulled an arm back to swing the PROTEC. With the rager almost on top of them, the girls collapsed to the ground, rolling into defensive balls. The rager was three feet away when Vince snapped the PROTEC forward, the metal sack catching the man at the sternum with a ragged crack. He went horizontal, tumbling hard onto the sidewalk, his head bouncing on the concrete. Vince widened his stance, prepared to swing again. He'd struck the man so solidly that he was sure he'd shattered his ribs. Perhaps even killed him.

The rager shook his head, eyes milky and confused, blood streaming down his neck, and they both looked up when they heard the whirring. A police drone was hovering ten feet above. "Stay on the ground," a grainy voice commanded. Ignoring the aircraft, the man lifted to his elbows, let out another scream—this one in agony as much as anger—and tried to stand up. A tracer dart connected to a thin cable shot out of the drone, catching him in the abdomen with 50,000 volts. He quivered in seizure, falling backward.

Vince stood over him, hand wrapped around the PROTEC, ready to spray or swing again if he rose. Danny and the boys inched forward, but Vince motioned to stay back, instructing them to run into the dojo if the man got up. The two girls, crying loudly, scampered back into the store. Within a minute, two police officers arrived on Segways, handcuffed the unconscious form, and took vital signs to ascertain he was alive. They checked the man's ID. "Jesus, this guy's a doctor," one of the policemen said in surprise.

A camera on the drone and the multiple cameras mounted on the buildings had filmed the incident, and the officers had been monitoring the action on screens mounted to their Segways as they headed toward the location. "Nice job," one said to Vince. "The PROTEC's badass."

An ambulance arrived. The boys and several parents surrounded the site. The policemen continued to circulate through the crowd, taking video statements from anyone who witnessed the attack. The girls crept out of the store and took turns thanking Vince.

"Dad, that was so cool," Danny beamed.

Vince didn't know how to respond. Nothing felt warmer than a son's admiration, but he was devastated by the boy's new normal. "Danny, it wasn't cool. The man was sick, and I'm sorry I had to hurt him."

Danny nodded. "I know, but it was awesome. You should have heard the guys when you knocked him out. You're a hero." He swung his arm right to the left, mimicking his father, making a sickening *thunk* sound.

Vince thought it important to turn this into some kind of teaching moment. But he was tired and, more than anything, disgusted at society's amazing ability to adapt, embrace raging as just another obscenity to be tolerated.

After dinner that night, as part of their Saturday evening tradition, he and Danny sat in the den to watch The Happiness Network. The streaming service, which only broadcast positive, family-friendly fare, had quickly overtaken Netflix as the preferred viewing destination. People lived enough violence and were no longer interested in watching it for entertainment. Vince had introduced Danny to the mindless comedies he used to watch in reruns at his son's age: *Gilligan's Island*, *Happy Days*, *The Brady Bunch*, and old movies infused with compassion and optimism: Disney films, and anything starring Adam Sandler, John Candy, or Steve Martin.

Danny was amazed by the programs' most mundane aspects: The idea that kids gathered in malls and malt shops, attended high-school football games, or rode their bikes while neighbors protectively watched over them. A life free of violence, plagues, environmental disasters, and political unrest—the very life Vince had once taken for granted—now seemed like science fiction.

That night after he'd put Danny to bed, Vince couldn't sleep. He replayed being overwhelmed by panic and adrenaline as he intercepted the rager. He could hear the thud of the man's ribs caving, like a terrible song stuck in his head. At 4:00 a.m., he gave up any hope of slumber and quietly padded into the kitchen to make coffee. Inadvertently, he whipped his arm forward as he walked, reliving the feeling of the PROTEC making contact, a pleasant shudder vibrating his body. He fantasized about what might have happened if the man had not gone down, swinging the PROTEC back and forth, pummeling the rager, the wet smack of metal meeting flesh, until he stopped himself, feeling like he'd been caught doing something very wrong.

The next day they headed to Washington Park for their Sunday morning ritual, which they both referred to as "church." Vince had abandoned any man-made explanations of a higher order—it was difficult to comprehend a god these days—but he did seek a sense of spirituality, and he wanted Danny to explore some kind of meaning. They crossed through metal detectors to enter the fir-lined paths of the gated park. The collision of nature and a sense of security had a profound effect. People smiled and stopped to chat and socialize in ways they couldn't outside of the refuge, and Vince was thrilled to see Danny experience normal human interaction. He encouraged his son to smile and greet other people. He wondered if lack of contact was the problem. It all seemed to start when large groups inexplicably became filled with hate, distrust, and conspiracy theories, espousing violence as opposed to conversation and compromise. Had this somehow opened the gates to raging, as if the societal immune system had been weakened by cruel discourse, allowing the infection of violence to spread? Perhaps the solution was as simple as spreading kindness.

The next day, as he walked from his car to his office, he was still buzzing with the pleasant sensation he had experienced at the park, and he offered a "good morning" to the parking lot attendant. He'd passed the man daily for three years, but neither had ever said a word, instead both offering occasional nods. The attendant had a middle eastern complexion, and Vince realized he might be guilty of racism. He'd assumed that the man didn't speak English, or in any case, had no interest in talking to a customer of his skin tone. The attendant frowned, unsure of what Vince had said, then uttered a quiet "morning" in return, his eyes fixed on the ground.

Vince offered the greeting to three other strangers as he approached his building. The first ignored him with a grimace, but the other two excitedly returned the salutation, flashing surprised smiles.

At the intersection of the alley and his building, he saw the old lady. She was here every morning: a graying woman of indeterminate age, wrapped in a tattered red blanket, even on hot days. Most of the time, she stared at the park across the street as if watching ghosts. A crude cardboard sign scrawled with HELP AN OLD WOMAN was perched behind a metal bowl, which held a few coins and dollar bills. Begging had become a difficult endeavor, people retreating or cowering from anyone approaching them. But on a few occasions, Vince had dropped change into the receptacle, receiving an appreciative nod. Today he reached into his wallet for five dollars and knelt at eye level. "Good morning, young lady," he said brightly. The woman's face flashed fear as he drew near, but when she saw the bill, she mouthed a silent thanks.

The next day Vince stopped at a Peet's Coffee on his way to work. After the massacre at the Salt Lake City Starbucks two years earlier, people had stopped communing in coffee shops, so most locations had been modified to become drive-thru, coffee slid under bullet-proof windows. He ordered three large lattes, yelling a happy "good morning" to the baffled girl behind the thick glass.

He consumed one as he drove, clumsily exiting his car in the parking lot, balancing the two remaining drinks. He approached the parking lot attendant. "Good morning," he said with a smile. "Hey, I hope you like coffee."

The man looked confused as Vince held out the cup. "For me?"

"Sure." Vince smiled. "It's a latte with pumpkin. Probably a million calories, but I figured it's the season. You know, I just wanted to show a little appreciation for the great job you do," Vince stammered. "I hope you like coffee. I wasn't sure, but..."

The man took the cup. "Good," he smiled as he took a sip, then took another and laughed. "Really good."

Vince looked at him and realized he'd never seen him smile. "Great. Well, enjoy."

He was walking away when the attendant yelled, "Thanks again." Vince turned. "That was nice of you. Have a great day."

Vince was elated as he approached the woman by the alley. As always, she was swaddled in the red blanket. "Good morning," he said, dropping to one knee as he handed her a coffee. "I brought you a latte. With pumpkin spice." The woman narrowed her eyes with suspicion. "Hope you like it," Vince said. She relaxed a bit, took the drink, and nodded a thank you.

That night he related the experiences to Danny. "I think we should try a new approach," he said. "Let's be the nicest people on earth. Greet everyone with a smile. Be generous. Kind."

"Dad," Danny said skeptically. "If we start yelling hello at everyone and buying them coffee, people will think we're nuts, and we will go broke."

Vince smiled. "Some people will think we're nuts, but maybe we can start something. What if everyone started being nice? If you can catch the raging virus, maybe you can catch a nice virus."

The next night at dinner, Danny was anxious to tell his father about his day. "Dad, I tried it. I smiled a lot and said good morning and good afternoon to everyone. I gave Lisa Duncan one of my cookies."

"And how did it go?"

"A few people looked at me like I was cuckoo," Danny laughed and twirled his fingers by his head. "But a couple smiled and said hello back. Lisa Duncan said my cookies suck, but she seemed happy and gave me her apple."

"That's a good start," Vince said. "Keep it up."

That night Vince went to bed with a long-forgotten sense of optimism. Perhaps with a nudge of kindness, the disease could burn itself out. Maybe Danny would someday live a normal existence. But in the early hours, he woke abruptly, his pillow soaked with sweat. He leapt out of bed engorged with energy, as if he might explode. Slapping the sides of his head hard with both palms, he felt the urge to put a fist through the wall as he replayed the thud of the PROTEC tearing into the rager, wishing he would have kept swinging, over and over, until the man's body was pulp. Nobody would have blamed him for killing a rager. He stared at the bedstand, where he left the PROTEC at night. He imagined grabbing it and heading out into the street. Perhaps there was another rager somewhere out there he could put down, and this time he'd make sure he never got up. He craved the sound and sensation of metal balls meeting bone. Vince shuddered himself back into reality, trying to chase the violent thoughts out of his head, like an alcoholic refusing a drink. He visualized Danny, the happy parking lot attendant, kind people returning their greetings. Clad only in his boxers, he walked into the backyard, the chilly air shocking as he did jumping jacks to relieve the energy. When his mind calmed, he headed back to bed but lay awake most of the night, confused and terrified by his thoughts, wondering if this was how the infection began.

The next morning he took Danny to school, feigning a headache to avoid talking to the boy. He was riddled with shame but also felt as if he were on the verge of a terrible anger he craved. After dropping Danny, a car pulled out in front of him unexpectedly, filling Vince with anger. He leaned on the horn and gunned forward, almost rear-ending the BMW. Veering into the opposite lane next to the car, he considered crashing into the vehicle. They were on a hillside, and there was a good chance he could force the BMW off the road and down a steep ravine. Vince smiled at the thought of the car flipping end over end, perhaps bursting into flames like they did in the movies. Then he looked over to see a young woman hunched over the wheel, a baby seat strapped in the backseat, giving him a terrified glance that brought him back to reality. He accelerated past the BMW and took the next freeway entrance to avoid having to look at her again.

At his office, the parking lot attendant gave him a cheerful wave and yelled, "Good morning." Vince wondered what the man really wanted. Perhaps since Vince had given him a coffee, he expected some kind of gift every day. Maybe if Vince did not give him things, he would vandalize his car, or worse, attack Vince. He did not look like he could be trusted. Vince reached back on his belt to finger the PROTEC. He considered bringing it out to teach the attendant a lesson. A surge ran through him as he visualized the man falling to the ground, metal balls puncturing his body. Vince stopped for a moment and closed his eyes to enjoy the sensation, feeling aroused. When he opened his eyes, the attendant was staring at him, backing up across the lot.

Vince hustled into his office, downing a glass of water while attempting to calm himself. He dialed Leslie, his ex-wife. She had moved two hours away to the coast and saw Danny every other weekend.

"Hey, surprised to hear from you in the middle of the week," she said. "Everything okay?"

"Uh, yeah," Vince lied. "Well, not really. I've got a bad situation at work, and I need to go out of town for a couple days. An emergency.

Do you think you could come and get Danny after school? Keep him till I get back."

"Vince, I can't bring him in every day. He'd miss school," she protested.

Vince fought the urge to scream at her. Why couldn't the bitch just do what he asked? He visualized using the PROTEC on her. Rearrange that cute blonde face. Then, horrified by his thoughts, he said, "Leslie, I really need you to do this. I'm sorry, but I have no choice."

Leslie heard an unfamiliar strain in his voice. She knew her ex well enough to understand he wouldn't ask if it wasn't important. Despite their differences, Vince had always been a devoted father and adored Danny. "Sure, Vince. He can miss a couple days. I'll take care of it. Listen, are you okay?"

"Yeah, fine," he answered abruptly. "Thanks. I'll call you when I get back."

He opened a desk drawer and brought out a small metal box, placing a thumb on the fingerprint reader to unlock it. Two years earlier, when the gun ban had gone into effect, he had opted to break the law and keep two weapons: a 12-gauge shotgun hidden in the back of his closet at home and the Glock sitting in the box. Both guns had been inherited from his father, and neither had ever been registered. To justify the decision, he assumed some of the ragers would keep firearms, and he had no intention of bringing a PROTEC to a gunfight.

The Glock felt like a natural extension of his hand as he snapped in the clip. There was a pleasant tingle as he envisioned firing the gun. It would be a public service to go rager hunting. Perhaps he should start with the parking lot attendant. There was something off about him. He looked out the window and watched people walking in and out of the buildings. He could go right to the courtyard and catch them all by surprise. Empty a clip, then reload on the way to the parking lot, where he would take out the attendant and whoever else was around. He envisioned the 9mm slugs tearing into bodies, spattering red holes as people flew backward. Pocketing two additional clips, he shoved the Glock into the waistband under his jacket and headed downstairs.

As he exited the doorway, he saw the woman in the red blanket staring as if she could see through him. He momentarily felt embarrassed, then considered starting with her. She was part of the problem. The filthy homeless had been the original ragers, first littering the streets with garbage and feces and used needles before they began attacking people. They'd probably spread the disease like rats. He considered whether he should use the Glock, or perhaps pull the PROTEC to take her down. One well-placed swing to her skull should do the trick. Save the bullets for more difficult targets.

The woman looked fearful, but rose, dropping the blanket, and Vince realized she was much younger than he had thought. His right hand traced to his hip to find the PROTEC as she kept approaching. When she reached him, she placed one hand to his face, embracing him around the waist with the other as she pulled him closer. Vince initially recoiled. Her lips neared his ear as she kept repeating, "Just think love. Relax. Just think love."

Vince visualized Danny's face, then sunk into her embrace, his hand slipping away from the PROTEC to pull her closer. The Glock dug into his ribs, and he wondered if he should pull it out, place it in his mouth, and pull the trigger.

ANNEMARIE

In retrospect, I never should have put that snake in Annemarie Kitsap's mailbox. It wasn't like it was a rattler or cottonmouth. Nothing that would jump out and fang you. Just a big bull. Ferocious looking, but harmless. Prized in these parts for their propensity to devour rodents and truly dangerous reptiles.

In my defense, I meant no harm. Regard it as a romantic gesture, the clumsy flirtation of a love-struck kid. Truth is, I always adored the girl. Even before she inspired that warm tingling down south, I'd stare at her all googly-eyed, captivated by the curly red hair that shot out her head like a forest fire. Skin too white and pure to sprout from this hot county. Porcelain features so sharp she appeared otherworldly, like a beautiful gift from aliens.

From birth, Annemarie was a force of nature, attacking life as if it owed her more than the rest of us. By the time she was four or five, adults were afraid of her. Instead of cooing about what a pretty child she was—and there's no doubt she was the most beautiful little thing anyone had ever seen—they'd circle as if approaching a foamy-gummed Rottweiler. Annemarie cared less, so self-assured she didn't require hugs or affection. At Sunday Services, when a visiting pastor said, "My, what a stunning young lady," Annemarie looked at him as if he'd just passed gas in an elevator, muttering, "Tell me something I don't know, Jesus-man."

Our spread bordered the Kitsap's farm, and since Annemarie and I were only a year apart, our folks threw us together whenever they were feeling neighborly. Annemarie regarded me with the disdain of an angry older sister, acting as if my mere existence was God's plan to annoy her, but I happily accepted her eye-rolling and sucker punches, thrilled to be in her sphere, her insults and outright cruelty just fueling my love. A happy cuckold by age four.

I was Jane Goodall and Annemarie, my rare primate. I observed every aspect of her progression. I marveled as her rail-thin, little-girl body retracted and expanded in all the right places, and she abandoned her farmer jeans for a tight denim uniform that served as inspiration for me as I trailed her down school hallways. Sometimes I'd sneak through the soybean fields that separated our farms and climb into the sweetgum tree that afforded a view of her bedroom, transfixed by the Annemarie bedtime ballet, straining young eyes to catch the entire performance. The delicate way she removed her clothes to be replaced with one of four t-shirts I knew by heart. My favorite: her dad's old white wifebeater, barely covering those hopeful breasts. Her hair-brushing ritual, red silk freed to drape soft shoulders. Finally, she'd prop herself up in bed for twenty minutes to read before the room went dark, and I'd rush to the library the next day to find whatever was of interest to her on the remote chance she wanted to engage in a literary discussion.

I could write a bestselling book called *The Wonderful Taste and Aroma of Annemarie*, detailing decades of covertly inhaling her strange and delectable scents. Johnson's Baby Shampoo wafting off those Shirley Temple locks when we were toddlers. The tang of cinnamon from the wad of gum she'd sometimes rip from her beautiful mouth and shove into mine, seemingly with malice, but an act that gave me indescribable pleasure. The sour, sensual aroma of her armpits when she'd roughly throw me into a headlock to deliver an Indian rub. When I was nine, she tackled me behind the barn after her folk's anniversary party, pulled up her gingham dress, and peed all over my head—an act meant to humiliate, but to this day one of the greatest experiences of my life.

Annemarie's perfume evolution: her mother's *eau-du*-something in grade school; the sweet trace of Charlie that defined her junior high years; the Spice Girls Body Spray in high school; and finally, Dior J'Adore, the signature spoor of a more adult Annemarie. Throughout this progression, I was her constant Secret Santa, saving up my scant allowance to leave gifts by her locker.

But my devotion and attentiveness seemed lost on her. I knew someday she'd understand our inevitability, but teen years are difficult. As we aged, Annemarie's attitude toward me morphed from disdain into outright hostility. I remember her yelling, "Get away from me, you goddamn freak," during sophomore year, when I took my usual seat on the bus behind her, a spot chosen to afford the perfect vision of her elegant ears. After that, when she saw me, her face would screw with hate, and she'd extend a hand as if to shield herself, which devastated me more than you can imagine. At one point, she inserted family into our relationship. One day when I returned from school, my folks were waiting for me. "Annemarie's parents complained. Leave that girl alone," Dad ordered.

But, of course, that was impossible. *And ridiculous.* I looked forward to the day when the Kitsaps were family, and we could all have a laugh around the dinner table over Dad's silly order. I knew our fates were intertwined but could understand how others might have difficulty comprehending the relationship.

What I really needed to do was regain her attention, which wasn't easy. There were so many distractions in Annemarie's world. A girl so beautiful and brilliant is assaulted on multiple fronts by people that can't help but desire her. And that's when I came up with the snake idea.

As little kids, we played together in Felt Creek, capturing tiny water snakes and transporting them to a bigger pool to watch them wriggle to freedom, sometimes even racing them like slimy racehorses. Though Annemarie didn't share my complete fascination with all things reptile, I admired the fact that, unlike every other female I'd ever met, she was fearless about creepy crawlers.

And so putting the big bull in her mailbox was just a playful love pat, a reminder of the good times we'd experienced together. Yes, a bit of a jolt, and perhaps in the back of my mind, I was enacting a little revenge, but it was the kind of thing I was sure she'd appreciate. I was prepared—even wildly anticipating—retribution. I stuffed the snake into the oversized receptacle and retreated behind a tree across the road to see her reaction.

But I'd forgotten that Annemarie's old grandmother was visiting from Sevierville and watched in horror as the old bat hobbled out to check the mail, probably hoping to discover her Social Security check or perhaps an advertisement for a *Hoveround* power chair. Annemarie was always the one to retrieve the letters, and it never occurred to me someone else would open the box. I wasn't in a position to see the old lady's face, but as she flipped open the door, I heard her scream, "Lordy," an old folk curse around here, then she stumbled hard, falling flat on her back. The snake was as surprised as she was, probably half-insane with fear in the hot metal jail, and it sprung out, landing flat across Grandma's legs. As the ancient gal raised her head, the bull crept up her stomach and slithered across her face to escape.

I'd heard the term "stroked-out" but had never witnessed it. The closest I'd seen was in seventh grade, when Dennis Sticka had an epileptic seizure. He was at the chalkboard, stressing out as Mrs. Geller tried to get him to conjugate a verb, and then suddenly he's on the ground, shaking like someone hooked jumper cables to his nuts and frothing something fierce. Grandma's mouth stayed dry, but she vibrated in place just like Dennis.

Annemarie was thirty feet behind her and dashed forward when she heard the scream. She watched the snake slide over the old woman's body and saw me turn and dash into the forest, terrified that my practical joke had put an old woman in her grave.

Some good news: Grandma lived, so I'm not a murderer, although her face is frozen in a crooked scream. She also lost the ability to speak, though she did develop a grunt-based language that her family understands. From what I remember, she wasn't a big talker anyway.

But the episode left me quite unpopular with the entire Kitsap family. Within an hour, the Sheriff was knocking at our door, and I had trouble coming up with an answer when Daddy asked, "Why in the hell would you put a snake in someone's mailbox? What in God's name is wrong with you?"

"Annemarie," I wanted to scream. "Annemarie is what's wrong with me." But I knew he wouldn't understand. Nobody could.

My folks and I had to appear before a judge, and I was fearful that I might be sent to the boy's prison in Dandridge. I'd heard horrible things about what went on in that place. My mother always described me as having "fine features," which I knew in prison was synonymous with "hello, little bitch, come give your daddy a kiss," so I wasn't looking forward to incarceration. Luckily, my attorney managed to convince everyone that a strict boarding school would be a better option, and it was decided that I'd travel four hundred miles to attend Fork Union Military Academy, with the stipulation I never return home until I was at least eighteen and that I maintain a hundred yards between myself and any Kitsap for the rest of my life.

Can you imagine never being able to get within a hundred yards of Annemarie? I call that cruel and unusual punishment.

After the proceedings, Mr. Kitsap jabbed his dirty farmer's finger at me and said, "If I ever see you on my property, I'll shoot you down like a dog with rabies." I figured he was just trying to impress Annemarie with his best Atticus Finch impression but made note that I needed to avoid their farm when he was around.

Annemarie's attitude was more distressing. I'd hoped she might see this for what it was: a misguided attempt to gain her love. Instead, as we walked out of the judge's chambers, she slid a hand to the back of my neck, pulled me close, and whispered, "I'm going to kill you. Not right now. Maybe not this month or this year, but I will kill you." She dug those beautiful nails into my neck till blood ran down the back of my shirt. It was terrifying, and I felt myself grow hard.

Fork Union Military Academy beat prison, but not by much. It's a place constructed on rules—which runs counter to my personality—and I hated the silly uniforms. It made me feel as if they were planning to refight the Civil War, and we were the first line of defense. I wasn't raped, though there were a lot of disgusting consensual sins committed in the woods surrounding the place. On holidays my family would come to see me since I couldn't go home. It made my mom cry when we had to spend Christmas at the Fork Union Days Inn. When I'd politely inquire about Annemarie, she'd get this hopeless look on her face, her tears flowing even harder. But I couldn't stop myself from asking.

They offered to come get me when I graduated, but I told them I'd take the bus. I didn't mention my little detour. I'd heard from my sister that Annemarie was a freshman at Austin Peay State in Clarksville. It had been over three years since I'd seen the girl, and I was hopeful that by now our issues would be forgotten, replaced by mutual yearning. I was excited to let her know I'd be attending Austin Peay in the fall, even prepared to suggest we could share an apartment.

I hadn't anticipated the difficulty I'd have finding her. I thought I could wander around campus, our reunion appearing happenstance. *Wow, Annemarie, how are you? I didn't know you went to school here. I'm just checking out the place since I'll be coming here in the fall. Sure. I'd love to have lunch. Stay in your dorm tonight? Yeah, that would be great, as I'd just planned to grab a cheap motel.*

But there were almost ten thousand students, and I needed to do some detective work to find her. I knew she was an English major, so I chose a discreet spot in front of the liberal arts building, knowing she'd come by sooner or later. Sure enough, at around 3:00 p.m. I saw her exiting a side door.

"Well, look who the cat dragged in," I yelled in my most energetic and mature voice, though to this day, I've no idea why I picked such a hackneyed greeting, like something you'd hear from an eighty-year-old-geezer surprising a war buddy at a Rotary luncheon. Nervous, I guess.

Annemarie was walking with two friends, those adorable lips in mid-giggle, when she saw me. Her reaction wasn't as I'd hoped, her eyes flashing from fright to rage. "What are you doing here?" she screamed. "You stay the fuck away from me, you creep. I will call the police. You're not allowed anywhere near me." She and the other girls turned and hustled toward a back parking lot. I didn't want to cause a scene, so I casually followed at a safe distance. They jumped into an old Tercel, Annemarie driving, and I made note of the license as they sped away.

Of course, this was a major setback to my plans. It was obvious that Annemarie still harbored resentment. I needed to take action to get our relationship back on track. I'll admit that my solution wasn't ideal, but when is an eighteen-year-old in love ever rational?

That evening, I borrowed a pillowcase from the Motel 6 and hiked to a swampy field outside of town, gathering up all kinds of snakes. Nothing dangerous, but a collection that would impress the most seasoned herpetologist: a thick corn snake, several bright water snakes, even an eastern hog-nosed snake. The next afternoon I was back on campus. It only took me a few minutes to locate Annemarie's car, which I was pleased to discover wasn't locked, probably because there was absolutely no reason for anyone to break into the thing. I did find a gym bag stuffed behind the driver's seat and paused to zip it open and inhale my love's tart aroma. My plan was to release the snakes in the car, which might jolt Annemarie out of her angry funk and return her to better times. I was leaning across to the passenger seat, just about to dump the bag, when I heard her voice.

"I told you I was going to kill you," Annemarie said, her voice surprisingly calm, considering what she was about to do. I assume I'd be quite tense right before I shot someone. When I saw the gun, I lunged sideways but was hard to miss from three feet, trapped within the confines of that little car. The first bullet, which was probably aimed at my head, caught me in the right shoulder. The second was much more lethal, coming in right below my belt buckle, tearing up my insides.

And that was the last time I ever saw my beautiful Annemarie. She pushed her head into the car as I lay splayed across two seats, snakes slithering in the blood pooling on the passenger floor. "I told you," she said, assuming she'd killed me.

But that's ancient history, though certainly the defining moment in my life. The little .32 caliber bullet is still lodged a fraction of a millimeter from my spine, governing my existence. The doctors say it can't be removed and warn me that someday it'll likely shift and kill me. But dying might not be so bad, since living as a paraplegic doesn't have a lot going for it. They moved me back to my parent's farm, confined to my bed, with an occasional foray in a heavy metal chair. Dad died five years ago, so Mom must attend to me, cleaning up my piss and shit, just like when I was an infant. The cheerful soul I remember has morphed into a sad old woman that cries before she dozes off. I know because I require very little sleep. I lie here late at night, listening to my mother's agony.

And later, when it's very quiet, I concentrate hard. Sometimes I'm sure I hear Annemarie, a quarter mile away, home for a visit, getting ready for bed. Annemarie pulling on that T-shirt, thumbing through the books on her shelf. And later, as she reaches to turn off the light, I sense that she's thinking of me, regretting all the tragedy that's come between us. Right before she dozes off, I can hear her mouth a sweet, "Good night, my love," as she pulls the covers to her chin.

A VERY BRADY FUNERAL

GREG TOOK THE RED-EYE from Philadelphia to LAX, hoping to avoid the scene that was now unfolding as he approached the baggage claim.

"Hey! Greg Brady."

He shuddered, picturing what would come next. Two older women, probably sisters, and one of their college-aged daughters suddenly broke into a sketchy song, accompanied by some ill-conceived Midwest white woman dance steps. "*Here's the story / of a man named Brady / who was busy with three boys of his own,*" they sang, before applauding and doubling over in laughter. Brady karaoke. They used their hands to frame boxes around their faces, trying to replicate the iconic tiled opening of the show. Cell phones were being ripped out of purses and pockets, a small crowd moving tighter around Greg.

He smiled weakly, pulled his baseball cap down a little tighter on his famously floppy locks, gave a little wave, and soundlessly mouthed, "How ya doin'?" and tried to be friendly—*Brady's were taught to always be friendly.*

"I don't think I would have made it through adolescence without your family," a bulimic silver-haired woman told him, grasping his elbow intimately, as if she were sucking some power through Greg's arm. He attempted a caring smile and patted her hand, noticing gray eyes that appeared accustomed to pain. "I couldn't stand growing up. Oh, my God, the stories I could tell you." She shuddered as if a freezing wind was blowing through the terminal. "I'd lie in bed or hide in my closet and pretend you were my family just to get through the day."

A little girl pulled at his arm. "Are you someone famous?"

Suddenly there was a tickle on his left ear, hot moist blowing, the unmistakable protrusion of bullety breast implants against his shoulder, then a familiar aroma that left Greg wondering if they still made Charlie perfume. A woman in her fifties, dressed in a kaftan that allowed for maximum cleavage while camouflaging her true proportions, was leaning into him, whispering. "Greg, you're the Brady I most wanted to fuck. I used to touch myself when I watched the show."

"Good to know," Greg mumbled as his bag slid down the chute. *Thank God.* He grabbed his suitcase and rushed out the door, thrilled to see his brother pulling up in a dented Volvo station wagon.

"Hey, aren't you the famous Greg Brady?" Bobby laughed as he leaned out his window, cameras flashing as the crowd trailed them onto the street. "Look," he yelled. "It's the star of *A Very Brady Christmas* and several episodes of *Hollywood Squares*."

"Jesus, a woman back there told me she used to masturbate to the show," Greg said with disgust as he slid into his seat.

"Creepy," Bobby grimaced. "Though I'll admit I occasionally like to rub one off while watching reruns of *Celebrity Apprentice*. You know, Meatloaf and Joan Rivers. That would get anyone hot."

Greg barked a laugh and squeezed Bobby's neck. "Good to see you, bro. You always know how to make me laugh. Thanks for picking me up. I could have taken an Uber."

Bobby patted his brother's knee. "What? When you can be squired in a fine vehicle like this?" He motioned around the car, which seemed to float on a patina of crust. Fast food wrappers and Starbucks cups blanketed the floor, the carpet strewn with tiny pieces of copper wire and screws. Greg grimaced as he picked up a stained four-month-old copy of the *LA Times* and tossed it in the back seat. "Careful. I haven't read it yet," Bobby cautioned. "Anyway, it was good to get out of the house."

"I bet." Greg bit his lower lip. "How's the grieving Brady clan?"

"As you might imagine. Marcia's using the situation for creative inspiration, lots of drama. Jan isn't saying much, she just fawns over her kids, and Cindy's been sitting in the backyard drinking boxes of Pinot Grigio and smoking a lot of weed."

Greg fished a pair of sunglasses out of his pocket. The people in the car next to them were staring.

"Seriously, Cindy's been on her cell phone all morning. She has a podcast, and she's doing a special episode from the backyard. Have you heard it? I think it's called Direct from Bradyville. She actually has a couple sponsors: Depends and a drug that makes you pee. Or stops you from peeing. Not sure." Bobby honked a couple times, then abruptly switched lanes without signaling. "Have you noticed our fans are elderly?" he continued. "Hey, maybe you could have your own line of incontinence supplies, or a special Greg Brady Hoveround Scooter. You could be the next Wilford Brimley." Greg backhanded his brother on the side of the head. "Anyway, Cindy's show is an hour of trivia from 1970s television. People call in. Lots of obscure television trivia. What was *Kojak's* middle name? Which family pet did Greg Brady lose his virginity to?"

"Fuck you," Greg laughed. "Speaking of moms, how's Carol?"

"Carol is…well, Carol. Gotta give our step-mom credit. Eighty-seven years old and still kicking ass. She's upset but holding it together. Oh, she has a new boyfriend. Edward or Eduardo, some kind of elegant spic name. He looks like the little Chihuahua that used to sell tacos, only slightly taller and not as funny. Thinks he's Ricardo Montalbán. Has a cheesy little mustache and wears ascots. I'm not shitting you. Apparently played a bad guy forty years ago in a couple Burt Reynolds movies. And not the good Burt Reynolds movies like *Cannonball Run II* or Hooper. He's young. Probably only seventy-five. Mommy's a cougar."

Both men smiled and then grew silent. "I can't believe it," Bobby muttered. "Peter. What the hell? A stupid way to die."

Greg reached up to pat his brother's shoulder, then flopped his head back against the headrest, reaching up under his sunglasses to squeeze the tears threatening to roll down his cheeks. "Bobby, we did what we could. He hasn't been right for thirty years."

Bobby suddenly veered sharply to the left in a barrage of horns, nearly clipping two cars to exit onto Lincoln Boulevard. "Hold on, we have company." A black SUV was forced by traffic onto an adjoining road, with a photographer hanging monkeylike out the back window, his fist wrapped around a long-lensed Nikon. "Get ready," Bobby warned. "Paparazzi. Everyone is very interested in the Bradys again in our moment of tragedy. Oprah called Carol. Wants to do a one-hour special. She told Carol we're America's family, and the country needs to know we're okay."

"America's family," Greg repeated. "America just wants to pry into our lives."

Bobby nodded. "I know you hate this but buck up. It's only for a couple days. Be that adorable Greg Brady that all the kids used to masturbate to."

~

IT HAD BEEN BOBBY that called Greg to give him the news. Greg had just arrived at his office at West Chester University, where he taught in the Film and TV Department. Three decades earlier, he'd abandoned LA, choosing a small town outside of Philadelphia where he could remain anonymous. In the early days, he was a campus celebrity, but now most of his students had never seen *The Brady Bunch*, preferring entertainment that featured superheroes, vampires, and zombies, viewed on iPads. When his cell phone rang, he brightened.

"Good morning, little brother. Six a.m. on the West Coast. A little early for you. What's happening?"

"Greg, bad news." Greg could tell from his tone that this was serious. Bobby was the relaxed one in the family, always enjoying a joke, floating through life like it was all one hilarious sitcom.

"I'm just gonna say it. I'm at a hospital. They brought Peter here last night. He was in a coma, and he died about thirty minutes ago."

"What?"

"Not kidding. He was appearing in this crazy event last night. A radio station in the valley sponsored it. It was supposed to be a phony boxing match at a sports bar. Battle of the child stars. He and Danny Partridge. They were wearing headgear and big gloves, but something went wrong. Danny clipped him pretty hard, and he fell back and hit one of the posts and was knocked out. They brought him here. Put him into a coma to relieve the pressure in his brain, but it didn't work."

"I don't understand. He was fighting Danny Partridge? Danny's a black belt in karate. Peter couldn't fight Mrs. Howell."

"He needed the money. They were paying him a thousand bucks. He's been having a tough time. I didn't want you to know because it would just upset you. He hasn't been able to find work, so he's been doing all kinds of crazy things. He was going to the convention center in Anaheim once a month to appear with a bunch of old TV stars, selling pictures and autographs for ten bucks a pop. He's in a low-budget television commercial for a Toyota dealer in Paso Robles. And he was drinking a lot. Maybe doing coke again. He was in bad shape."

"Jesus, Bobby. You should have told me. I would have brought him out here."

"C'mon Greg. This has been going on for as long as we can remember. I kept trying to get him to move in with me, but he refused. Peter was stuck in the memory."

Greg nodded. Like Springsteen sang, "Glory Days."

He hung up and made plans to return to LA for the first time in a decade. He'd hoped he would never have to go back, especially for a funeral.

Now, THE TWO SWITCHED to small talk for the rest of the drive, Greg marveling at how crowded LA had become since he'd lived here. When they pulled up to the old Brady home, the house that was emblematic of the 1970s ranch burger, Greg felt as if he were thirteen years old. As Bobby warned, there were vans and camera trucks parked in front, several paparazzi blocking the sidewalk.

"Greg," a guy yelled from behind a video camera, "Does this mean war with the Partridges?"

"Any truth to the rumor that Peter actually overdosed on heroin?"

"Greg, do you want to comment on the rumor that you and your sister Marcia actually have a forty-year-old son who works as an Uber driver in Florida?"

Greg stopped for a second, feeling the urge to pop the faces behind the camera, but Bobby gripped his elbow and kept him moving. Jan met them at the door, hugging Greg for a long time, until she passed him off one by one into the arms of his sisters. The Brady Bunch were now approaching elderly status, but to Greg, it felt the same as it did fifty years earlier: Jan soothing and sad; Cindy, pigtails long gone but still smelling of spearmint gum; Marcia, still looking remarkably like the 1974 version, staring at him with oversized eyes.

He finally made his way to Carol, still wearing her pixie haircut, a wrinkled version of his television mom. Greg sank into the tiny woman, realizing how much he had missed this embrace. As she led him to the couch, he looked around the room, marveling that it hadn't changed. A Brady family museum, the hip sixties decor had fallen into the decorating dregs for a few decades but had now emerged as the height of stylish again. He smiled at the big open staircase, perhaps the most photographed stairs in television history. Somehow, Carol managed to keep the furniture looking almost new.

The family spent the day in quiet conversation, rotating between tears and occasional laughter as they related their favorite Peter stories. Late in the day, Alice and her husband Sam arrived from

San Diego. As they all sat down for dinner, Alice started serving the family. When Carol objected, she wagged her finger at her former boss. "Mrs. Brady, it makes me happy, so please just sit down." Carol and Alice started discussing logistics for the funeral, the Brady kids nodding and agreeing as if they were once again teenagers.

"Tomorrow is going to be sad and stressful," Carol announced. "There will be a lot of people at the funeral and a lot of press. It's important that the Brady family handle this whole thing with dignity. I know we are all confused and maybe even angry, but we have to maintain."

That night Bobby and Greg decided to continue the teenage illusion and sleep in the bunk beds in their old room. "Jesus, this place is a time capsule," Greg said in amazement as he looked around at the GI Joes, cowboy action figures, and Matchbook cars lining the shelves. "It's like we never left."

Bobby smiled and grabbed a towel, placing it at the base of the door to block the crack, then grabbed one of the dolls and popped off its head, reaching inside the body to pull out a joint. "Care to smoke some forty-five-year-old weed? I got it from Bobby Sherman in 1973 when he guest starred on the show. That dude was a serious head. And by head, I mean he had an incredible head of hair."

"Jesus, are you kidding me? I seriously doubt you can get a buzz from that. It's probably mildewed."

"Nah, I'm kidding, it's not that old," Bobby said as he lit it and passed it to Greg. "I was here last Thanksgiving and hid some for a rainy day. Sure feels like it's raining right now." They sat on the floor in front of an open window, blowing smoke into the night air, careful not to catch the eye of anyone out front. Most of the photographers had left, but there were still a couple leaning against a rusted Toyota, hoping for a shot of the grieving family, preferably a major breakdown.

"What a crazy life," Greg said. "Who would have thought when the show went on the air almost fifty years ago that we'd be sitting here like two old men in a bedroom that's a shrine to our childhood? It doesn't feel right without Peter."

"That's for sure." Bobby tapped ash into an empty Coke can. "Now we're two short of a bunch."

Bobby popped his head back as if returning from a dream. "I have an idea." He jumped up and began rummaging around the top shelf in the closet. Beaming at his discovery, he brought down a Daisy Red Ryder BB gun.

Greg laughed as he turned off the lights in the bedroom. Leaning out the open window, they took turns taking shots at the Toyota. The two men were smoking from vape pens at the front of the car and turned to look at the side when they heard the ping of the BBs hitting the metal. They glanced around, unsure of what was happening. On the fourth shot, the rear window shattered, and the Bradys giggled loudly as they closed the window.

For the next two hours, they lay in the tiny beds. "Greg, why do you think Peter couldn't get away from it, but you did? Hell, Professor, you went off and forgot all about being a TV star. Don't you miss it?"

"Not a bit," Greg whispered. "I just wanted to live a normal life. I'd never go back. What about you? You've stayed in LA, but you turned out relatively normal."

"Not everyone would agree with that." Bobby chuckled. "But why would I want to be a celebrity when I can run Bob Brady's Home Automation and pay alimony to two ex-wives. Anyway, I didn't stay handsome enough to be a star. Peaked at age ten. But I was one cute kid." He mugged. "Without doubt the cutest of the Brady's. Luckily nobody recognizes me now."

The next morning, after one of Alice's big breakfasts, the family climbed into three limousines and headed toward The Burbank Congregational Church. A huge facility adept at hosting celebrity funerals, the entry was roped off with plenty of security. A gaggle of photographers descended on the limos as they pulled up, a hundred or so "Bradyiacs" and gawkers gathering around the perimeter as well.

There were over two hundred invited guests, many of them television stars from the 1970s. Greg thought it looked like a *Love Boat* plastic surgery clinic, many so medically enhanced it was like entering a parallel Hollywood universe. Donny and Marie were in the fourth row, Melissa Gilbert was sitting on an aisle, and three or four cast members from *Happy Days* were near the back. Greg recognized several faces he'd seen but couldn't identify peppered throughout the crowd.

The service was short. Hollywood folks like events condensed into sitcom-length sound bites. Afterward, most of the crowd migrated to a reception room behind the church. Greg and the family lined up to shake hands and hear nonstop funny or touching stories about Peter. After the crowd had thinned, the family noticed most of The Partridge Family seated about fifty feet away, with Danny Partridge the only one conspicuously missing.

"Wow, ballsy of them to show up," Marcia whispered to Greg.

"It's not their fault." Greg pulled her tighter. "It was an accident."

There had always been a close but turbulent relationship between the families. While *The Brady Bunch* was more popular than *The Partridge Family*, impish Keith Partridge's quick rise to "teen singing idol" caused competition between the kids. Keith was suddenly on the cover of *Rolling Stone* and performing in front of stadiums full of screaming little girls, while Greg and Peter were relegated to stories in *Teen Beat*, clean-cut relics of a different time. The Bradys tried to cash in on the family band craze, donning pasted polyester jumpsuits in some kind of adolescent Elvis-homage, and recording an awful album, but the family's complete lack of musical talent squashed their dreams of becoming America's new singing sensation.

But now the competition was forgotten. Shirley Partridge, propped up with a cane, led her family to the receiving line, starting with Carol. The two embraced and began to cry. Keith Partridge hugged the Brady girls, finally making his way to Greg.

"Jesus, Greg, I don't know what to say." Keith pulled Greg toward him. Greg was stiff at first, but finally gave in to his embrace. There was an androgynous doll-like softness to Keith—even an aged Keith—that made you want to be close to him. "Listen, buddy, how about we get a drink?" Keith motioned toward the bar. "I'm sure you could use it."

The two grabbed glasses of wine and retreated to a back table. Keith pulled his chair close to Greg's, their knees touching, leaning in as if to shield them from the rest of the crowd. "Greg, I'm so sorry. And I am sure this is the last thing you want to hear, but Danny feels terrible. He wanted to come but thought it was inappropriate. But really, his prayers are with you."

Greg nodded. "Thanks. We don't blame Danny. Neither of them should have been there."

"Thanks, Greg. You know, this is so strange. We've both been through so much. It almost feels like we're all part of the same family. How are you doing? You look good. I heard you're a college professor?"

"Yeah, a little college in Pennsylvania." Greg felt a familiar twinge of admiration seeping up. Keith had always been one step ahead of him. The sex symbol. The rock star.

"Can you believe it?" Keith smiled. "Look at you and me. We're eligible for Social Security. Where did the time go? It seems like just yesterday we were eighteen and partying with the Bay City Rollers. How'd we get so fucking old?"

"The years flew," Greg said, feeling a hand on his back. He swiveled to greet a disheveled man with a red beard wearing a black beanie.

"Just had to offer my condolences, Greg," the man said as if greeting a good friend. "Man, this is awful. I'd just seen Peter four or five months ago. We did this episode of *Ellen*, kind of a 'where are they now?' We had lunch, and he was terrific. You know, everyone loved Peter." He turned to Keith. "Keith, great to see you. We should talk. I think you and I are both up for that Time Life infomercial, and I was thinking we should do it together. Wouldn't that be a killer? The two biggest heartthrobs of the seventies on one stage."

Keith smiled and shook his hand. "Sounds interesting. Let's grab lunch."

The man made a peace sign, tapping his chest above his heart. "Greg, you know I'm here if you need anything."

"Who the hell was that?" Greg asked.

Keith smiled. "C'mon, you remember Leif Garrett."

"That was Leif Garrett? Holy shit, he looks like a crackhead Russian taxi driver. Jesus, I wouldn't have recognized him." Greg glanced around the hall, suddenly wanting to leave. Go home and walk in the woods, have dinner with normal people. "Keith, it's great to see you. Really. I better get back to the family." He began to rise.

Keith jumped up, grabbing Greg's elbow and looking around the room, motioning at someone with a nod of his head. "Greg, give me one more minute. There was something I wanted to talk to you about. I know this isn't the best time, but since we're all here…"

"I'm so sorry about Peter." He looked up to see Rueben, the Partridge's long-time agent. He had to be close to ninety years old now, and Greg was surprised he was still alive. He had on huge black-framed glasses so windshield-thick Greg marveled he could see out of them, sporting a pastel suit with a loud floral tie, the stub of a hot dog-sized cigar poking out the pocket.

Greg reached to shake his hand. "Rueben. Wow. Great to see you."

Reuben plopped down in the chair next to him. "I know, kid. Too long. It broke my heart when I heard about Peter. He was a good kid. You know, in the old days, I used to try to get him to let me represent him."

Another man sat down at the table. "Greg, I hate to talk business on such a sad occasion, but I did want to bring you some really good news," Rueben continued. He motioned across the table. "Meet Dan Plummer. Dan's been really excited to get together with you." Greg gave Keith a baffled look as the man reached across the table to shake his hand. "He's responsible for some of the biggest hits on television. *Cajun Blood.* You know that show? Huge hit on the Outdoor Network."

Greg shook his head no.

"Ah, you'd love it. It's a reality show about a family that lives in an old box car in a swamp in Louisiana. They hunt alligators. Two of the cousins are married, you know, to each other. One of the daughters is missing her left arm. Some kind of birth defect, though the rumor in the show is that an alligator bit it off. She's got this stump covered with Voodoo tattoos. And she's a psychic. At the beginning of every episode, she tells someone's future."

Greg shook his head. "Sorry, don't know it."

"How about Dan's other big hit, *My Three Dads*. It's on what, Bravo?"

"Right, Bravo. One of their most popular shows," Dan replied.

"It's really touching," Rueben continued. "A reality show about two gay guys and a lesbian that live together. Maybe they're married? Can you do that now? I know gays can marry, but three? I can't keep up with all this stuff, but God bless America. Anyway, the gay guys are like your typical gays, but the woman, she's tough. What do they call women like that?" waving a hand at Dan.

"Butch," he said. "Dresses like a man. Drives a truck. Wallet on a chain. That kind of thing."

"And they're raising this teenage kid," Rueben continued excitedly. "He's in high school, and he likes to...wadda' ya call it, Dan?"

"He's a transvestite," Dan replied. "He competes in cross-dressing contests."

"Imagine that." Rueben snorted. "This kid—and he's good looking too, looks a little like Johnny Depp—dresses up in women's clothes. But he likes to bang girls. Then he goes home to his three dads, one of which is a dyke. Who wouldn't want to watch that show?"

Me, Greg thought, but nodded.

"All you need to know is that this man is the best." Rueben pointed a wrinkled digit. "He's got the magic touch. And guess what? He wants to put that magic to work for you. The Bradys and the Partridges. He's got a great idea for a show."

"Thanks," Greg said, waving a hand, "but I'm not interested. I'm retired from television."

"Retired from television? That's crazy," Rueben scoffed. "Television retires you. Greg, listen to the idea. This will be big. Bigger than *The Brady Bunch*. Lots of dough. You guys will be stars again."

"I appreciate the offer, but I'll pass."

"Greg, hear me out," Dan interjected. "You know what's happening in Detroit?"

"You mean that it's crime-ridden, broke, and has poisoned water?" Greg asked with growing annoyance.

"Exactly," Dan smiled. "And the Michigan film board is paying production companies to come there to boost the local film economy. So, we shoot there practically for free. Get this," he said, leaning in excitedly, "The Brady Bunch and the Partridge Family go to Detroit and move into a big old mansion the city has agreed to give us. The plot is that the two families are on the down and out and go to Detroit for a new start. They move in together—just like on the original *Brady Bunch*. Maybe we'll even do that same opening, but instead of your family, it's the Partridges and the Bradys. You'll live in a huge estate. Plenty of room for the two families. Even grandkids. And here's the incredible part. They're also going to give you guys businesses to run, all free. They've offered a record shop, which could be great. You and Keith running it together. Imagine how much fun that would be. There's even a little stage in the shop where they used to let bands play to promote their albums. The Partridges could play there."

"A record shop," Greg said sarcastically. "Isn't there a video store available?"

"Hey, it doesn't have to be a music store. That's just one idea. How about a medical marijuana shop? They also have a Dodge dealership. Imagine you and Bobby selling cars. And Dodge is a hot brand now. You don't like those businesses, we'll find something you do like. Maybe something a little risqué? They have a lot of topless clubs in Detroit. You could run one of those. Break character a bit, like Tony Soprano. Bada Bing. At night you all get together at the mansion, compare notes about the day. Who knows? Might even be a little romance. You and Bobby are single. Have you seen Laurie Partridge lately? That girl has aged nicely."

Greg looked at Keith to see if the idea of pimping out his sister was eliciting any reaction, but he just smiled.

"So let me get this straight," Greg said. "You come to my brother's funeral to pitch me on quitting my job, pretending that my family is broke and can't find jobs, and moving to Detroit to sell cars or albums or maybe run a strip club, while living in a house with the guy that killed my brother? Maybe screw his sister if all goes well? And you're going to film it all for the world to see?"

"Jesus, Greg, I thought there were no hard feelings about Danny," Keith said in a hurt voice. "Not cool."

Greg turned to face Keith. "There's a big difference between no hard feelings and cohabitating. Are you really in favor of this? It's nuts. Degrading. Do you want the world thinking you're so hard-up you need to move in with us and sell cars?"

"It is nuts, Greg," Keith answered, "but that's what sells right now. I think people would love this show. And I'm sorry, but there is big interest right now, given the tragedy. We need to strike while the iron is hot."

"He's right, Greg," Reuben added. "This is a huge opportunity. It's important for both families. Everyone wants to do it, but they knew you'd be the holdout. We need you. Don't you want to help your family?"

"You mean you've discussed this with them, and they're in favor of it? I can't believe that," Greg said with disgust.

"I met with them yesterday," Dan said. "Lots of details to be filled in, but everyone's on board. Even Alice."

Greg shook his head in disbelief. Then he glanced across the room. His family was standing together, staring at him, pleading smiles on their faces, all yearning to be The Brady Bunch again.

THE 100-YEAR-OLD SHERIFF

LET'S PUT *ME* IN perspective. The year I was born, that horny bastard Woodrow Wilson was elected to his second term as president. Four million Americans took a European vacation to fight in World War I. The federal income tax doubled—from 1 percent to 2 percent. Women couldn't vote. The Klan was a respectable organization that enjoyed stringing-up black men like bloody Christmas ornaments.

I was twenty-five when I shipped out to fight the Japs in World War II. Before we began our love affair with Toyota, we had a hell of a war with the Japanese. They killed a lot of my friends, and I reciprocated.

My son Egan died of old age. My daughter Kathleen was killed in a car accident during the Nixon administration, burned to a crisp in one of those Chevy Corvairs Nader warned us about. I probably buried my wife before you were born. My point is…I'm old. Really goddamn old.

I didn't get to be ancient because I eat a lot of kale, or meditate, or take all the vitamins they're always peddling around here. Like it or not, it's mostly the luck of the gene pool and the ability to move fast when something comes flying at your head that gets you to centenarian status.

So drink up and screw while you can. That's my credo.

My father was seventy-nine when he was killed in a bar fight; otherwise, he probably would've outlived me. He was putting a good whooping on a couple reprobates that were breaking up his tavern—

Pa, hell on wheels with his Louisville Slugger—when one of the cowards shoved a knife into his neck.

Two men lost their lives that day: Dad and Dick Owens, the bastard that killed him. Course, Dick took longer to die. The judge gave him twenty-to-life in Deer Lodge, but since I had a few hard friends serving time, Dick's sentence ran two weeks and three days. He was shivved in the rec yard, one of my pals chanting, "Bucky Ryan sends his regards." Don't think I'm the kind of man that sends others to do his dirty work. I just couldn't figure a way to get my hands on Dick Owens.

I was a fierce boy, raised on thirsty land that pretended to be a cattle ranch outside Hysham, Montana. In 1930, my folks moved into town when Dad bought the Brunswick Bar.

I developed a love of beer and rodeo, and after high school, I went on the circuit trying to make my name as a bull rider, which is about the silliest profession a man could ever pursue. A life of broken bones, bad checks, and more than one case of weeping dick.

I have to thank that son-of-a-bitch Hirohito for my transformation. I was a degenerate, heading for a short life of ill repute, when the draft came calling. You can't tell now, since my body's been rusting away for the last three decades, but I was a big, fearless bastard. I found salvation in the Marines—men just as crazy as me—but the Corps gave us a sense of discipline and purpose. For the next two decades, I was all *semper fi*, fighting my way across the Pacific. I even spent time in Vietnam when things were just heating up before deciding to take a military pension and come back to Montana to do a little hunting.

I'd married Lacey in 1950. She was a good old gal, and I figured I owed her a permanent home. Our daughter was born in '53, and we wanted her in a good school, so we moved back to Billings. I have an aversion to the indoors and found a job working as a warden for the Montana Fish and Game. It didn't pay much, but it kept me in uniform and carrying a firearm.

Time speeds up as you age. Next thing I know, Kathleen's gone, cancer takes Lacey, and I'm forced into mandatory retirement. With two government pensions, I didn't have financial worries, so I bought a camper shell and lived a nomad's life, wandering around with a shotgun and a fishing rod until I finally got so fragile I had to move into this goddamn place.

Rimrock Retirement Village. First thing, it's not a village. There's no town square or cute café. This is a warehouse for the soon-to-be dirt-napping. A place to stick grandma without feeling too guilty.

The food's okay, as long as your palate favors soft. There's a physical therapist—damn pretty, too—that works with me three days a week in the little gym. While I'm worthless from the waist down, my arms are in good shape, and she helps me lift weights and stretches me out. She wears a white cotton shirt, and sometimes I get a whiff of sweet young woman that makes me feel young again.

The place has made me smarter. I never took to books, but Rimrock's filled with them, and now I go through two a week. Often there's a lecture during lunch. Maybe a professor from the college or a mouthy expert on something. I'm well-versed on the Sauropelta dinosaurs that lived in Montana one hundred million years ago, and I can give you a fair accounting of the events leading to Custer's Last Stand.

And I've turned into a bit of a geek. Unlike most of the retirement zombies that fear any technology more complicated than a coffee maker, I'm competent with my computer. Hell, I even surf a little porn now and then.

I've built a nice relationship with Bart, the techie kid that comes in twice a week from the high school to help us communicate. Nobody wants to make an old-fashioned phone call anymore—or God forbid, actually visit—so if a resident wants any contact with their family, they're forced to go digital. You should see these sad old faces light up when they get a text from their lazy-ass son or an email from a granddaughter too damn busy to come by.

My legs are useless sticks, but Medicare bought me a Hoveround Power Chair, and I paid extra to upgrade to the fanciest model. I've always driven American vehicles, and the Hoveround is made in Florida, which is almost America. An old-fart's Jeep, it has four-wheel-drive and knobby tires. I go for long drives around the neighborhood. Folks are good about giving a wide berth to a hundred-year-old man scooting down the bike lane. If the weather is favorable, I'll drive three miles to the VFW to down a scotch with a fellow vet while I recharge the batteries. Course, my wandering puts me on the shit seat with Rimrock's management.

"That thing isn't an automobile, and you can't be driving around city streets," Linda Thatchett—or Nurse Ratched, as we call her—tells me, wagging a disapproving finger. "You're going to cause an accident." At my age, I have no use for rules, but I don't want to get hit, so I strap a six-foot fiberglass rod with one of those fluorescent warning signs on the back of the chair, and I install a bicycle headlight to make myself more visible.

Truth is, I've been rubbing Linda wrong since my third week at Rimrock. She'd just taken over as the Village Manager, as she likes to be called, and it started badly. My pecker is past its prime, but I still appreciate the female form, and when a buddy at the VFW told me about a pole dancer from Shotgun Willie's that offered senior discounts for in-home performances, I was quick to schedule a visit. I had no idea Rimrock had such strict visitation rules. When Cinnamon (probably not her real name) showed up, I introduced her as my great-niece, figuring it plausible I'd have some Puerto Rican blood in my lineage. She cranked up some howling music and had stripped down to a piece of red floss when Linda burst through my door. You should've heard the ruckus she made, threatening to throw me out. Jesus, it wasn't like I was going to fornicate with the girl. Seems to me it's my room, and I should be able to do anything I want. But time's not on my side, and I don't want to waste it shopping for new accommodations, so I do my best to stay out of Linda's way.

Of course, every village has an idiot, and this place is no exception. About a year ago, I was having lunch with Claire Davis when she complained about the new aide, Randy Belmont. "A thief and a bully," she said, nose scrunching. "He bosses me around. Says demeaning things, and I know he took my pearl necklace. Plus, I'm missing some of my dainties. The man's a pervert."

You might notice that the elderly can be paranoid, maybe something to do with our senses slipping away. When you can't see or hear very well—or even keep a clear thought—it's easy to imagine all kinds of nefariousness.

But Claire's sharp as a tack. And even though I had a hard time imagining why anyone would want to steal her big old underwear, I decided to investigate the situation. Sure enough, several other residents were missing stuff. Frank Gaspar couldn't find the Hamilton watch he'd inherited from his father. Ellen Bass was missing a diamond ring and two bras. Pete Fromm was frantically searching for his gold Elk's Club cufflinks, and he told me the two hundred in cash he always kept in his drawer for beer and gin rummy was sixty bucks light. Seemed like there was a veritable crime wave going on in our little village.

I started keeping a close eye on Randy and discovered Claire was right. When nobody was looking, he was a cruel bastard. I watched him giggle after he banged poor old Steve Amick into a wall while transporting him in a wheelchair to the clinic. Another time he screamed, "Shut up, you old retard," at David Long when he thought they were alone. Poor old David is so far gone he didn't take offense, but I sure did.

I could have gone to Linda to report all this, but I suspected old Nurse Ratched would just try to cover things up. Plus, this was personal. This is my community, and I'm not going to stand for foolishness. That's when I anointed myself the Village Sheriff.

First, I needed evidence. I ordered one of those fake Rolex watches from eBay, and at lunch, I was flashing it around, making sure Randy saw it. "I thought I'd lost this a year ago," I said all feebly, "but I found it in my sock drawer. My wife gave it to me in 1966 for my fiftieth birthday." Randy's eyes lit up, and I knew what he was thinking. If my old brain was so rotted I could lose the watch once, it wouldn't be surprising if it disappeared again.

I had Bart show me how to use the camera on my laptop, and I set it up on my bed stand so I had a good view of the whole room, then put the Rolex out in plain view. When I got back from dinner, it was gone, and when I checked the video, I had a nice clear movie starring that thieving bastard Randy.

I kept my old steamer trunk from my days in the Marines to use for storage and as a coffee table. It's packed with handy stuff from my military and warden careers I thought I might need someday. That night I cracked it open to prepare for the mission. Then I called my buddy from the VFW, Dave Hawkins—Dave's a Navy guy, which normally drops a man a few notches in my estimation, but he was a Seal in Vietnam. I'd had occasion to work with the Seals, and there was no better outfit in the military. Dave was in his late seventies now but still a big, mean son-of-a-bitch. He also drove a cherry 1978 Dodge van. I was going to need that.

Randy parked his filthy Toyota Tercel in the back lot, which was pitch black after the sun went down. The next evening, I had Dave pull his rig next to Randy's car. We were perched in front of his van, presumably just shootin' the shit, when Randy came out. He gave us a startled look, probably guilty over stealing my fake family heirloom, but I'm sure he thought we were two harmless skeletons.

"Hey, Randy," I said in a cheery voice as I rolled toward him. "I've got something to show you." When I was a warden, one of the go-to items in my truck was a Miller Hot-Shot cattle prod. Sometimes I'd have a run-in with a vicious ranch dog, or a feral pig. Five thousand volts has a calming effect on even the most aggressive animal. Randy was just about to unlock his door when I pulled the cattle prod up from the side of my seat, placed it square on his nut sack, and hit the power. He howled like a wounded coyote and fell to the ground, jerking around like he was having an epileptic fit, followed by a powerful smell that indicated he'd filled his pants. I moved the stick to his neck and gave him a little more juice while Dave cuffed his arms behind his back and shoved a rag into his mouth. Dave pushed him through the side door of the van, helped me into the passenger seat, and stuck my chair in the back. Randy was squirming around the deck, eyes bulging as he tried to scream. I gave him another couple zaps to the leg and told him to "hush up and stay still."

I knew Randy lived alone in a little dump on Howard Avenue. I'd checked out the place on Google Earth and saw he parked his car in a dark driveway beside the house. Dave pulled close to the side door. Randy was upright now, and I warned him, "You do anything silly, and I'll jam this thing up your bunghole and fry you till the top of your head blows off." Dave pushed back his jacket to reveal a little .38 strapped to his belt, which enhanced the threat.

I'd borrowed latex gloves from the nurse's cart and handed a set to Dave. Dave set me in my chair, used Randy's key to unlock the door, and shoved him into the house. It was just the kind of place you'd expect a reprobate like him to inhabit; filthy dishes stacked high, pizza boxes and beer bottles littering the floor, and a sour odor, like someone had pissed the couch.

I kept an eye on Randy while Dave searched the house. "Bingo," he yelled, carrying out an Amazon box filled with old folk's memories, including the missing watches, Pete's cufflinks, and Claire's necklace. I recognized yellow diamond earrings and a gold bracelet that poor old Peggy Peterson used to wear before she passed away, plus a wad of other jewelry.

Under the bed was a stash of prescription drugs he'd stolen, enough meds to start his own pharmacy, if his clientele primarily suffered from high blood pressure and the inability to pee.

To top it off, his bottom drawer was stuffed with old women's underwear. Claire was right, he was a pervert. I'll admit to having participated in a few strange sexual scenarios—especially during my days in Southeast Asia—but this guy's peccadilloes baffled me.

Randy was sitting cross-legged on the living room floor, hands behind his back, when I held up a pair of the panties. "You're one sick bastard."

He got a wild look, jumped up, and bolted for the front door. It was a clumsy move, him being handcuffed. I hit the forward joystick on my Hoveround and stuck out the prod to trip him. He went flying into a bookshelf, his head smacking so hard it sounded like a baseball bat meeting a fast pitch. I stuck the cattle prod against his cheek as he slid down, gave him a level ten zap, and he popped six inches into the air.

Dave rushed over, feeling around his limp head and neck. "Damn, Bucky, you killed him." He didn't seem upset, just curious.

I can't say I mourned Randy's passing. Seems to me the world has enough thieving, deviant drug dealers, but this did put a crimp in the plans. We just intended to get everything back and scare him out of town, not kill him.

Dave and I loaded Randy's corpse and all the stolen loot into the van. We straightened up any mess we'd made and left all the drugs on the coffee table. Then we drove twenty miles toward Roundup. I knew this area from my warden days. There was an abandoned spread with a dried-up well that hadn't been used since the fifties. I figured it would make a good final resting place. Dead weight's tough, and it took a lot of effort for two old men to get Randy's body out of the van and over the lip of that well. After we let loose, it was a couple seconds until we heard the thud, and we figured he was a good fifty feet underground in a place nobody would ever look.

Back in town, we stopped at a car wash and hosed out the back of Dave's van to get rid of any evidence. I even put the high-pressure wash to the wheels of my chair.

Randy wasn't the kind of guy that anyone missed, and it took at least a week before people started asking about him. When he didn't show up for work, and she saw his car in the lot, I suspect Nurse Ratched made a few calls. But a guy like Randy was soon replaced.

Every couple of days, I'd sneak a piece of jewelry into someone's room and let them find it as if it had just been misplaced. I mailed Peggy Peterson's granddaughter the earrings and bracelet, with a note that Peggy had left them with me for safekeeping. I tossed the underwear. It would be too hard to explain.

A detective eventually showed up. They had searched Randy's house, found the pharmaceuticals, and suspected he'd been involved in some kind of drug ring and had either gotten lost or someone had made him disappear. I added to the intrigue a bit when the cop talked to me. "He was a shifty one," I told him. "The day before he disappeared, I saw him in the parking lot talking to a couple tough-looking types."

I thought it was an Oscar-worthy performance. In any case, there was no way they'd suspect a hundred-year-old man. I assumed the Village Sheriff could go into retirement.

But that plan only lasted a couple months. One day I saw poor old Bonnie Campbell sitting by herself, cheeks damp and red. When I asked her what was wrong, it came rushing out.

"My granddaughter Becky has fallen in with the wrong sort. Poor girl got divorced two years ago. She's lonely and has two young ones to take care of, so she's vulnerable. All of a sudden, she meets this man—Mike Sutton—and she's in love." Bonnie spat out *love* like she was describing something you'd find stuck to your shoe. "Mike's a lazy SOB," she continued, "and moved in with her. Right away, he loses his job, and now spends his days drinking at that dump on Lewis Avenue, the 11:45 Club. Doesn't lift a finger to help or contribute a penny. Becky stopped by this morning to see me, and she had a big bruise on her eye. Wouldn't admit what was happening at first, but I know that girl, and she finally told me that Mike hits her.

She'd confronted him about the way he was looking at her daughter Emma. Girl is only fifteen, and Mike's been eyeing her wrong, making inappropriate comments about how 'she's becoming a woman.' Becky told him it had to stop, and he smacked her. Turns out he's drunk and mean most nights."

"Sounds like she needs to go to the cops. Get a restraining order," I said.

"That's what I told her," Bonnie said, getting more riled up. "She told him he had to leave. He said no way, hit her again, and told her if she called the cops, he'd kill her and take off with Becky. She's scared."

"The police know how to deal with those kind of men," I said. "They'll keep her safe."

"Do you really believe that?" Bonnie said sarcastically. "Women get beaten and killed all the time by men who aren't supposed to be there. I'm only sorry my husband Louis isn't around. He'd go over there and break Mike's neck."

I tried to make her feel better but knew I had to do more. I hold a special rage for assholes that take advantage of those who can't protect themselves.

So just like that, the Village Sheriff was back in business.

I'm Facebook friends with Bonnie, and sorting through her pictures, I found a shot of Mike and Becky. I figured he would be one of those people happy to friend anyone, and when he accepted my invite, I was able to dig into his background. It amazes me what you can learn about a man on the internet. He'd been a good-looking guy, but you could see the Budweiser toll. Mike changed jobs every few months, his employment always ending with derogatory remarks about his previous boss, the kind of person that gets unfriended by anyone with half a brain. His timeline was full of sexist and racist jokes, and pictures of overly endowed women. His contacts—mostly Grizzly Adams lookalikes—were an angry lot that taunted readers to "pry their cold dead hands from their guns," had affection for some dirty knucklehead named Kid Rock, and posted about hoarding gold and their hatred of Hillary Clinton. The 11:45 Club appeared to be his main hangout. There were at least a dozen photos of him taken there, blitzed and usually clinging to a rode-hard bar fly.

I knew the place, having stumbled out of there a few times in my younger days, and decided the thing to do was to have a heart-to-heart with Mike, maybe encourage him to move on. I called Dave to invite him out for a drink.

A few days later, he picked me up in his van after dinner. Course "after dinner" in this place is 6:00 p.m., and we headed to the bar. I had explained the situation, and Dave, excited about another mission, insisted on strapping on his little pistol.

I do not think the 11:45 Club has been cleaned since my last visit in 1996. We had been sitting in the back for an hour when I saw a person who had to be Mike stumble in. The way he moved, he might as well have had "asshole" tattooed on his forehead, yelling snarky greetings at the late-stage alcoholics holding up stools. He was a grimy bastard, already three sheets to the wind. He ordered a beer and headed toward a lonely poker machine in the corner.

I rolled toward him. "Hey, Mike, isn't it?" I said all friendly like. He gave me a surprised look (I am aware I resemble a rolling prune), then frowned with no recognition. "I'm a friend of Bonnie's," I said. "Becky's grandma. I met you when you stopped by Rimrock." That seemed to make sense to him, even though I had no idea if he'd ever visited. He mumbled some kind of greeting. "How's Becky?" I continued. "What a great girl. Hey, can I buy you a drink?"

I knew Mike wouldn't be the kind of guy to refuse a beer, and he sat down and ordered a Pabst. He also wasn't one that appreciates small talk with two gentlemen, so after his first sip, I got right to the point.

"Listen, Mike, I've got a proposal for you." He perked up. "I've heard your home situation isn't working out, and you've got a bit of a temper. Word is, you're the kind of man that enjoys smacking women. Worse yet, there's a rumor you might be a kiddy-diddler."

He frowned in disbelief and began to rise. "What in the hell are you talking about?"

"It's okay, because all we want is for you to leave town. Hit the road. Never contact Becky and Emma again. And if you do that without making trouble, we'll make it worth your while. We're prepared to give you some traveling money: $2,500. Get a fresh start. Find some new woman to beat up, or a youngster to rape. Maybe head down to Alabama. They're more tolerant of that kind of thing."

Mike snorted through a crooked smile. "Old man, you're crazy. I don't know what you're talking about. If that bitch Becky thinks you two will scare me, they're nuts too."

"You're not getting the full picture," I continued. "You've got two choices. We follow you back to the house, wait while you pack up your stuff, and give you $2,500 to get lost. I know Becky works the late shift at the hospital tonight, and Emma's taking her grandma to the movies, so we have to get it done right away so you don't run into them. Or there's option number two, which I don't think you'll like."

Mike laughed. "You're threatening me?"

"Yep," I nodded. "Option two is that we kill you and dump your body into an old well. Pour some lime to melt you into a yellow puddle. Tough way to face eternity, like lemon pudding. We'd prefer not to do that, but it would save us money. Your call." Dave nodded in agreement as if we were discussing the latest NFL standings.

"I gotta admit," Mike said in amusement, "you're the weirdest old bastards I've ever met. You don't look like you could make it to the corner and back, much less murder me. But you got balls."

"So," I asked, "you want the money, or do you prefer door number two?"

I could tell he was fighting back an angry reply when a dim light went off in his tiny brain. "You really got the cash?"

"Yeah, of course. But you don't get it till you're packed and ready to head out. We'll follow you to the house."

Mike thought for a second, then said, "Let's see the money."

"No problem. It's in the van. But first," I said, pulling a pad and paper from the saddlebag on my chair, "you need to write a little goodbye note to leave at the house. Just something like, *Becky, I got a great job offer to work on a rig in the Bakken but need to leave right away.* Make everyone feel good about your sudden departure."

Mike eyed me suspiciously as I held out the pen. "You definitely have $2,500?"

"Write the note, then we'll go to the van, and I'll show you the money. Then we head to your place." I repeated what to say as he scribbled with a third-grader's penmanship and handed me the paper. "Okay," I said, "follow us."

Dave led the way, with me rolling behind Mike. "It's in the glove box," Dave said as we reached the far end of the lot, motioning at Mike to crawl in the passenger seat while he went to the driver's door to unlock the van. When Mike leaned in, I pulled the cattle prod out of my bag and jammed it taint-high. He was surprised to have a steel rod shoved against his balls and whipped around to face me as the electricity hit, sending him into spasms. As he fell backward across the seat, Dave wrapped a steel garrote around his neck and pulled hard. Mike had drawn a knife from his pocket, most likely intending to steal the money and scare us away, and I had to stay back as his arm flayed. The prod had decent reach, and I kept the power on for thirty seconds while Dave choked the life out of him, finally rolling him into the van's cargo area.

"So, he was gonna take the money, maybe stick us, then go home and beat up Becky," Dave said.

"No doubt. This was our only choice. Parasites don't ever move on."

Dave found Mike's keys and walked around the lot, hitting the unlock button until we found his truck. While my legs couldn't carry me, I did have enough strength to push pedals, and Dave helped lift me into the driver's seat. I followed him to Becky's house. I knew she was working until midnight, and the movie didn't get out until ten, but I kept watch as Dave used Mike's keys to enter the house. Ten minutes later, he came out with an old duffle packed up with Mike's stuff, and I followed him out of town, toward Roundup Road to the abandoned ranch.

Once again, we grappled to get the body into the well, Mike thumping hard, most likely squashing Randy, who had to be ripe as a week-old avocado by now. Then we dumped his stuff and a twenty-pound bag of lime down the hole. Dave's son owned a junked car lot on the edge of town, and I followed him there. He had a key to the gate. We removed the license plates from the truck and pulled it to a spot to be stripped for parts and crushed the following day. We figured there are many reasons a guy like Mike might disappear, and nobody would be looking too hard.

Course, Dave and I agreed we were not taking the safest possible approach on these missions. Grabbing men out of parking lots is not a great idea, though Dave had done some recon to make sure there were no cameras. Still, we might have been spotted, but we decided it was worth the risk. Plus, if they did catch me, I wouldn't live long enough for a trial. The criminal justice system moves too slow to be a threat to a hundred-year-old man.

A week later, I checked in with Bonnie. "Good news," she said. "Mike took off to work in the oilfields a few days ago. And you won't believe it, but he left some money. Twenty-five-hundred dollars! Guess he felt guilty."

I'd been prepared to spend some cash that night one way or another and preferred it go to Becky. We'd left the note Mike had penned on the kitchen table with a wad of bills.

And I assumed that would be the end of my vengeful adventures.

But here I am six months later, perched in a dark alley, my Hoveround wedged between a rusting garden shed and a black plastic dumpster. I left the cattle prod at home and replaced it with my M1 Garand rifle. Did I mention I spent most of my military career working as a sniper, usually laying under rocks and bushes with my face stained green? The Garand served me well over the years, and it was one of the mementos I kept hidden away in my locker. Tonight, it's going to see some action again.

From here, I have a decent view through Eric Purcell's bedroom window. Eric's a stockbroker—actually, I guess he prefers the term "wealth manager." He specializes in working with elderly clients, including several Rimrock residents. Last week it was revealed that his true talent is embezzling. There's somewhere in the neighborhood of five million dollars missing, which is a pretty fancy neighborhood, mostly stolen from the meager retirement funds of old folks who need every dime they've struggled to save.

Eric had no problem posting a million-dollar bail, which he probably intends to skip out on. I suspect he moved the other four million to some beachfront banana republic where he can spend his days sipping piña coladas while laughing about how easy it is to rip off the elderly. Maybe if I put him down, he won't have a chance to move the money around, so the court will never find it, and the bail money can repay some of my friends. Who knows? Maybe Eric even has a life insurance policy that will help defray some of his evilness. In any case, this seemed like a "the sooner, the better" situation.

He lives less than two miles from Rimrock, well within the Hoveround's range. While the other two missions were risky, just driving to a man's house to shoot him is insane, so I decided not to involve Dave. I've been rolling over here the last few nights, getting a feel for the target. Eric is predictable. Lives alone, home by around 8:00 p.m., and stands right in front of his window to enjoy the night air as he takes off his watch and gets undressed for bed. It's been a long time since I fired a weapon, but this is an easy shot: fifty yards at a brightly lit target.

I screw on the surge suppressor that will make the crack of the rifle sound like a badly tuned Dodge and wait for him to appear. While the smell of the alley leaves a bit to be desired, it's a pleasant night with a westerly breeze signaling summer is on the way. The rifle feels like a long-lost child.

You might be the type that considers me a murderer, the world's oldest serial killer. But remember, I'm a product of a different generation. A hundred years ago, the sheriff might have been forced to use his best judgment and take the law into his own hands to keep people safe. Hang or shoot a man that has no possibility of redemption. Sometimes right is right, and you don't need juries to tell you so.

From this distance, one shot will do, then I will break down the rifle and stow it in my bag. I will roll a couple blocks through alleys, then turn onto the street that has a wide bike lane, flip-on my headlight, and make my way home.

You might even notice the cute old man in his wheelchair motoring down the road. "Look at that wrinkled codger," you might say. "Kind of late for an old dude like that to be out." You get to my age and people don't think you're capable of much.

They might be surprised.

RAPING THE GODDESS

THE BELL JET RANGER threaded the high rises from downtown to Santa Monica, swept north up the beach, then turned inland at Santa Barbara to weave through oak-covered hills blackened with the remnants of a dozen wildfires. The helicopter ride from downtown LA to the Santa Ynez Valley was a brisk thirty-five minutes. When they reached his property, Bishke instructed the pilot to slowly traverse his sixty acres. "Just look at that ranch," he said proudly to his wife, Stephanie, gesturing through a porthole at the 18,000-square-foot mansion. "Rancho Elaine," he purred, the property christened for his mother. The U-shaped home was flanked by two cerulean pools connected by a six-foot-wide stream and an outdoor entertainment area that rivaled a Vegas resort. He'd recently planted five acres of grapes, intent on producing his own Rancho Elaine Pinot Noir.

Anyone that hailed from a western lineage wouldn't refer to Albert's estate as a ranch, but Bishke thought the stable and thoroughbreds qualified it for the designation. Though he loathed horses—all animals, really—he loved to dress up in his version of John Wayne duds and announce with a bad western drawl, "Let's head out to the ranch."

Angel, his property manager, was waiting in the customized Gator to transport them to the house. As they passed the expanses of bushy lawn, Bishke had him pull over to inspect the grass.

He shook his head in disgust. "I see brown. More water."

Angel winced.

There were a multitude of reasons for the neighbors to hate Rancho Elaine, and Angel was the one that bore the brunt of their discontent. The construction noise had been ongoing for two years. The previous spring, increasingly rare rain deluged an exposed hillside, transforming it into a slick chocolate landslide that closed the road for two days. They'd been picketed by a group of environmentalists outraged they'd bulldozed a stand of ancient blue oaks. With over two hundred exterior landscape lights, the place glowed like a strip mall, masking the dark skies so coveted by locals. Between the house, the guest and staff quarters, and a barn big enough to house fifteen horses, rooftops covered over 50,000 square feet, leaving people to wonder how two part-time residents could justify barricading so much rich farmland.

But if there was a single issue that made Rancho Elaine a pariah, it was water. Central Coast residents were fearful of running out. Reservoirs were drying up. Farmers watched their wells plummet to alarming depths. The Governor mandated a twenty-five percent reduction in water usage, and most people responded like good citizens, pulling out lawns and water features, installing low-flow showerheads, flushing intermittently—*if it's yellow, let it mellow*—and allowing shiny autos to dull with dust.

But Bishke was oblivious. At a cost of $700,000, he dug two wells, boring 2,000 feet to suck the aquifer that fed all the surrounding acreage. Since it was a private system, he suffered no restrictions. Neighbors were astounded when he pumped millions of gallons to fill pools and an artificial pond, thousands of gallons of water evaporating away every day. There were eight bathrooms spread throughout the property, several featuring rain showers that wasted more water in five minutes than most residents used in a weekend.

But the main ire was reserved for the massive expanses of green. In an attempt to recreate a southern horse farm, Bishke had planted ten acres of thick Kentucky bluegrass. The three equines that could have easily been nourished with hay bales lounged on swaths of luxuriant lawn kept emerald by mechanized blast sprinklers.

Neighbors boiled in continual rage. They'd protested and petitioned to the county, to Bishke, to Angel, but to no avail.

"It's my fucking water," Bishke replied. "Keep the sprinklers pumping," he ordered Angel. "I want to look out my window and think we're in Ireland."

So Angel kept his mouth shut and the water flowing. *Caramba, que va*, he'd tell his wife. If Bishke continued to pay him twice what he'd made at his last job, he could tolerate any *patron pendejo*.

JOHNNY ARMENTA SHOVED HIS index fingers into his ears as the helicopter whap-whapped two hundred feet above his property, creating a vibration that churned the fillings in his teeth. The Fat Hollywood Fuck had arrived in a dust cone, terrifying all the horses in the valley.

Johnny was the one most impacted by Rancho Elaine. Third generation on forty acres of farmland that bloomed directly across the street from Bishke, he was the main recipient of the noise and congestion. He'd always been a "live and let live" kind of guy, accepting the development as inevitable. But now, the estate was a threat.

His biggest concern was the wells and the precious water. Perhaps it emanated from his Chumash roots, but Johnny regarded the planet as a goddess to be respected and worshipped. She's kind and generous, as long as you treat her with respect. The key is to replenish so the bounty remains perpetual. He knew if he pulled too much nutrient from his soil, he'd create a barren field, so he rotated crops to maintain healthy dirt. He'd eliminated all insecticides, determined not to poison the Goddess. When the drought hit, he spent fifty thousand dollars—money he'd borrowed—to modify his irrigation to the most efficient drip system available, so water fed then flowed back to the aquifer. Honor the earth. That's all the Goddess asked.

Bishke honored no one. Since he'd tapped the aquifer, Johnny's well had dropped by ten feet. He was running out of water. Fifty years of family history, crafting artisan tomatoes from this fine dirt, wiped away, so one man could surround his ridiculous castle with a moat and a golf-course-sized lawn.

The previous day, while irrigating, Johnny heard a bellow as the pump strained to find water, finally belching a sandy liquid flow. His heart sank, like a man who'd been given weeks to live. Now he spotted Bishke across the road, riding in his fancy golf cart as the sprinklers drenched his grass. *This man is the devil.*

Two hours later, the first of Bishke's guests arrived. His entertainment business relied on contacts and investment, and he'd found the best way to build both was by throwing ornate gatherings. Always on the lookout for fresh capital, he'd found willing marks among the wealthy retired businessmen who migrated to Santa Barbara. Everyone wants proximity to fame. Normally prudent folks were easy marks when approached with a glamorous movie investment, happy to ignore the significant risks in exchange for a meaningless executive producer title and a pretend friendship with a celebrity.

The caterers and florists were hard at work preparing an Argentinian asado. A margarita bar had been installed by the pool, and three thousand dollars in flower arrangements were being distributed around the grounds.

Bishke walked the estate with Angel, barking instructions to make sure everything was perfect. When they came to the pond, he instructed him to "fire up the pumps tonight." In Las Vegas, he'd admired the show mounted every hour on the lakes in front of the Bellagio featuring sprays of water that shot two hundred feet in the air, airborne liquid dancing to classical music, and attempted to recreate his own version on his pond with rotating pumps that sent streams of water skyward to Andre Bocelli's "Con te partiro."

Angel dreaded this more than anything. He hoped nobody's gaze was directed toward Rancho Elaine tonight.

~

AS DUSK SHADED THE valley, the estate came alive with lights. Johnny watched a line of fancy cars progress through his neighbor's gates. He heard a low hum of music and chattering laughter as he approached field number one, which sat directly across from the entrance to Rancho Elaine. These five acres birthed his most valuable crop, heirloom tomatoes that fetched a premium price at the farmer's markets, and it was crucial they received water tonight as the afternoon had been brutally warm. In fact, Johnny thought, every day now seemed freakishly hot, as if the Goddess were suffering a fever.

Opening a valve, he had a moment of trepidation, fearing the same strain he'd experienced this morning, but the water flowed smoothly. He walked down a crop line, relieved to see clear droplets flowing out of the drippers staining the thirsty dirt. Pulling out a flashlight, he crouched every thirty feet to inspect the small tomatoes. The juicy orbs were starting to show color, green flesh beginning the transformation to brilliant red, yellow, and orange fruit.

Twenty minutes later, the pump emitted a horrible belch, the ground vibrating as water ceased flowing. Johnny sprinted for the pump house as metal impellers screamed, the dry blades overheating. Slamming the off switch, he fell to his knees, gasping hard and praying it was just an air bubble. He waited a few minutes to restart the power. The pump hummed smoothly, but as he waited for water, there was a loud hollow thump. Johnny dropped his head and flipped off the power to save the pump. The water was gone.

He slumped to the ground, his back against the small wooden structure, and wept for the first time since his son had been born.

Within a few days, his fields would die. The land his grandfather and father had nourished and protected, land that had fed and clothed three generations, would soon transform into worthless desert.

There was a blast across the road, followed by blaring classical music. Johnny was stunned to see streams of water shoot a hundred feet skyward, colored lights tracing the dancing flow. The rotating pumps fired the liquid at varying angles to the rhythm of the music as the crowd cheered.

He rose, cursing Rancho Elaine. Bishke had raped the Goddess, and now he was laughing at her.

~

ALBERT WAS BEAMING AS guests congratulated him on the water show when Angel pulled him aside. "Sorry, Mr. Bishke," he whispered, "but Johnny Armenta, the farmer from across the street, is out front. He's very upset. His well has gone dry, and he's blaming us. I think you need to talk to him. Calm him down."

"What?" Bishke said, annoyed. "I'm in the middle of a party. Not my problem. Tell him to get lost."

"Mr. Bishke, I don't think that's a good idea. Johnny's a good man with many friends in the valley. I think you should have a word with him to smooth things over. Perhaps there's something we can do to help. Tomorrow we could get Carl out here from the well company to take a look. Maybe it's just a bad pump."

Bishke couldn't believe Angel expected him to leave his soirée to deal with some disgruntled neighbor. Since he'd bought this property, jealous bumpkins had come out of the woodwork to cause trouble. Here he was, transforming a dilapidated property into this beautiful ranch, but these people couldn't stand the fact that he wasn't a local. There'd been awful letters, and twice he'd been forced to hire a cleaning service to sandblast graffiti off his stone gates, foul threats from the nutty environmentalists that would sacrifice progress to protect a few trees and annoying owls. The last thing he needed tonight was some Mexican or Indian—whatever the hell Johnny was—making a ruckus in front of his guests. The guy just wanted money.

"All right, let's get rid of him," he said to Angel.

Johnny was standing to the right of the porch, staring at the water flying through the air.

He turned to Bishke in disbelief. "You dry up my fields so you can spray water at the moon?"

The man looked crazed, and Albert tempered his anger. Might be some kind of crackhead. Best to placate and move him to the other side of the gate.

"Johnny, Angel told me there is a problem with your pump. Sorry to hear that. How can I help?"

Johnny shook his head in disgust. "How can you help? You suck our water for your theme park. Pave over farmland so the little rain we get can't return to the earth. Plant grass that belongs two thousand miles away. I'll tell you what you can do. Shut down those sprinklers. Let the aquifer replenish. You're going to destroy it for all of us," Johnny screamed, waving his arms. "You've already destroyed me."

Bishke backed up. The man was demented. He eyed Angel, wondering if he'd intercede if Johnny attacked. Maybe not. These locals stick together, especially the dark-skinned ones. He glanced at the door, calculating the odds he could get through it before Johnny reached him.

The ground shifted, and Bishke fell sideways. "What the hell," he yelled, catching himself with his right hand. The earth was vibrating. Bishke jumped off the porch, sidestepping toward the road, figuring it must be an earthquake. Best to stay clear of any structure. But this was unlike any earthquake he'd experienced. There was no jagged rocking, just a pulsation, as if a subway train were passing below. And the sound. Barely noticeable at first, but it built. A moan growing louder, only to be drowned out by the terrified shrieks from the backyard as people dashed around the side of the house.

Bishke and Angel sprinted through the side gate as the guests, caterers, and staff pushed past. Bishke's wife was standing near the pool, screeching as she hopped in a spastic dance. Then they saw the snakes, ten or twelve black forms shaking at her feet. The entire patio was undulating, and Bishke realized he wasn't looking at his ebony Italian tile reflecting moonlight, but rather at hundreds of black reptiles slithering across the ground. The pumps that had been firing water were still operating, but instead of liquid, snakes were being blasted through the air, landing on the patio and in the pond and pools. Snakes swam across the water and slithered onto the walkways.

"What's happening?" one of his guests shouted. The man and his wife had crawled on top of a table, kneeling precariously as reptiles surrounded them. Snakes had been thrown onto the food and were sliding across salads and platters of meat.

"They're coming up the pipes," Angel said, pointing at hose outlets at the edge of the gardens, as a line of black snakes popped out and fell to the ground.

"Turn off the pumps," Bishke yelled, fighting the urge to vomit, as Angel hopped toward the switch. Bishke ripped a long pool brush from the wall, using it to clear a line through the reptiles to his wife. Grabbing her hand, he swung the brush in a sweeping motion four feet in front of them, snakes flying, until they reached the house.

"What is happening?" Stephanie screamed.

"I don't know. We must have punctured a snake den. Calm down, I don't think they're poisonous. I'll call an exterminator. I'll..." He stopped to watch Angel run through the gate, as more snakes wriggled down the path.

"They're in the house." She grabbed his arm and pointed at the dining room. Snakes were pouring out of the bathroom and across the hardwood floor. Bishke slammed the door shut, as shiny reptiles streamed over the side of the toilet, hitting the marble with wet thumps.

He grabbed his car keys, pulling Stephanie toward the front door. Snakes were bubbling out of a garden hose on the deck. They leapt across the steps and ran toward the Range Rover parked in the lot. Snakes wriggled through the gate and covered the driveway.

"Ignore them. They won't bite," Bishke yelled.

The SUV flattened dozens of the reptiles. Most of the guests had sprinted to their vehicles and pulled to the road, but a few were standing fifty feet up Roblar Avenue, ready to continue running if the snakes drew near.

Within twenty minutes, Highway Patrol and Sheriff's cars arrived on the scene. A deputy shining a flashlight ran toward the driveway then jumped when he saw the snakes. "I got the call but couldn't understand what they were talking about. Unbelievable."

Within an hour, they'd blocked off the road a half mile in each direction, moving the barrier back as snakes continued to cover the area. Generators and flood lights were brought out to illuminate the road and fields, while neighbors, press, and curiosity seekers that could stomach the sight surrounded the scene. The snakes spread like an oil slick, blanketing Rancho Elaine, then moving up the road to spill onto adjoining land.

Scientists from UCSB were brought in. They tramped around the fields in thigh-high rubber boots in amazement. "*Charina Bottae*," one of the herpetologists observed, "rubber boa. Fairly common, and they won't hurt you, but you don't see them around here. I've never seen this many. I didn't know there were this many in the entire world."

Curious scientists arrived from UCLA to inspect the house. They found boas stacked two-feet high as they poured out open toilets and slithered up drains and into the bedrooms. A casing on one of the wells near the barn had cracked, and hundreds of reptiles streamed up from the chasm.

"I'm getting the hell out of here," Stephanie told Bishke, "and I'm never coming back. Sell this place—fast—if you can find anyone stupid enough to buy it."

Bishke ignored her, transfixed and terrified by what he was seeing. He was concerned about the forty-million-dollar investment disintegrating in front of him, but this was something more cataclysmic. He stayed on the road all night, moving back as the reptile perimeter grew.

The next morning the county brought in loaders and dump trucks to scoop the creatures up and haul them to a deep pit they'd dug two miles away, where workers in hazmat suits doused the snakes in diesel before setting them on fire. By late afternoon more officials gathered at the site.

"It's getting worse," the sheriff told Bishke. "We've capped every pipe coming from the well, but fissures are opening. Your field is caving in. You'll probably lose the structures. We think the aquifer went dry, and the land is collapsing and opening up these dens. And now it's not just boas. On the south edge of the property, we're finding rattlesnakes. A lot of them. It's getting dangerous. We can't keep up with the infestation, and they're on the move, spreading out. We're evacuating homes."

One of the scientists, the de facto leader of the group, was leaning against the hood of a fire truck as Bishke approached him. "What the hell is happening?"

Exhausted, the man pushed himself up and shook his head. "Well, the scientific explanation is *I have no idea*. I've seen snake infestations before, but nothing like this. This is biblical shit. We're not alone. Take a look." He held his iPad out to Bishke, showing an image of a ragged, downed forest covered with huge black insects. "That's Novo Progresso in the Brazilian Amazon. Big logging area. Two days ago, a five-mile square patch was suddenly overrun with *Titanus giganteus*—Titan beetles. Big as a man's fist. They're incredibly rare, and they're pouring out of the rainforest, eating everything in their path. They keep coming. Just like your snakes."

"But that's nothing." He swiped to a new page, showing a map of Ohio. "Those dots indicate micro-quakes. Starting yesterday at about 7:00 p.m., the land between Columbus, Ohio, and Pittsburgh, PA—which just happens to be one of the biggest fracking areas in the country—started experiencing earthquakes, which fractured oil and gas lines. The whole region is on fire. Flames and poisonous gas are shooting out of the ground. If they don't get it under control, the entire area is going to look like the surface of the moon. They're abandoning entire towns. An American Chernobyl. And that's just the beginning. Reports are coming in from all over the world with crazy stuff. A river in Russia dried up, like someone turned off a spigot. A city in China was attacked by crows. Like a Hitchcock movie, millions and millions of pissed-off black birds swooping down. I'm a scientist, and I've based my entire life seeking the logical explanation for everything. But I've no idea what's happening."

Johnny had quietly stayed on the road all night watching the spectacle. "The Goddess has had enough."

Bishke and the scientist turned to him. "What does that mean?"

"We were never in control," Johnny said quietly. "That was an illusion. We're only here as long as the Goddess tolerates us."

Fifty feet away, a hillside shifted then crumpled, unearthing a three-foot-wide cavern. A wall of rattlesnakes toppled out, fell into the barrel pit, and began slithering to the road. Bishke watched them wriggle up the pavement, joining a shimmering wave, a bloody sun at half-mast behind the Santa Ynez Mountains.

THE PASS LIST

KATIE TOOK IT UPON herself to plan their seventh anniversary, hoping it might help elevate her out of the funk she'd been experiencing. She suspected that her husband, Robert, a prime catch from every traditional matrimonial metric, couldn't comprehend the desires that had recently overcome her. While she embraced their upscale suburban life, she craved a fluttering stomach, the wonderful unease of naughty. On Sunday afternoons, while Robert was sweating off a few sets of tennis across town, she'd fantasize about a different kind of mate, hollow-headed and brutish, her fantasy rooted in a monochromatic world where Ryan Gosling took her on the kitchen counter, car lights flickering twenty stories below. In reality, she knew bad boys were ninety percent heartbreak, while men like her husband, steady Eddies, promised a lifetime of security and love. But she felt driven to infuse a little fantasy into their lives.

To celebrate their wedding, she emailed a suggestive invitation to Robert to join her at a tony hotel suite. When he arrived, she was delighted that, per her instructions, he'd donned the Armani tuxedo she'd bought him for last year's Christmas party. Katie led him to the couch, her Pilates-perfected body draped in layers of Agent Provocateur to be slowly stripped away. Thirty minutes later, the Veuve Clicquot and oysters half-consumed, she proposed the game.

"As your gift, I'm giving you a pass list," she announced, tracing a toe up the inside of his thigh.

"A pass list?"

"Pamela told me about it," she said. "We each pick three people. People you don't know. Famous, like movie or rock stars. And if either of us ever gets the opportunity to have sex with them, it's approved. We get a pass."

"You mean my dream of hooking up with Hillary Clinton might actually come true?" Robert joked.

"C'mon," she said. "Be serious. Who are the three famous women you lust after?"

"I only have eyes for you."

"Nope. Play the game. What kind of woman turns you on? This is your big chance. You run into Scarlett Johansson in an elevator, and if it goes well, I'll give you a pass."

"Okay. I'll play, but you go first," Robert said.

Katie had spent hours considering her choices. "Hmmm, of course I'm turned on by guys that look like you," she said with false sincerity, "so I'll take Channing Tatum."

"Right. If only I was taller, younger, and very buff," Robert laughed.

"It's his eyes. Kind. Like yours."

"Thanks." Robert kissed her. "Next?"

"Your namesake. Robert Downey Jr. He seems fun," she said.

"Iron Man. Good one. And the final lucky man?"

"Ryan Gosling," Katie said with undisguised longing. "Hot. Not as hot as my husband, but…"

"Yeah. I get that a lot. When women find out I'm married, Ryan's their fall back."

"Okay, your turn."

"Let's see," he said, nodding his head in thought. "Maybe Charlize Theron."

"Nicely played," Katie agreed.

"And a crazy girl: Angelina Jolie."

"Wow, surprising, considering your vanilla Midwestern tastes." Katie playfully poked him.

"I'm a man of mystery," Robert said. "More exciting than you give me credit for. I might be a mild-mannered tax attorney, but I have some pretty good game. You're forgetting what a charmer I was when we met."

Katie peered closely at her husband, trying to see through the fog of intimacy. She had faint memories of their courtship, the lovely ache of new love highlighted by frenzied sex, but now they lived on different plains. "Robert, you're handsome and charming, but after seven years, I know you very well, and Angelina would tear you apart. Don't forget, she's the girl who wears her lover's blood in a vial around her neck. Like a vampire. But it's your list. So number three?"

"I'd go international. Penélope Cruz. If she's good enough for Javier, she's good enough for me."

"Not bad," Katie said, removing a layer of her outfit.

"So you're serious?" Robert smiled. "Anyone on our pass list is fair game? Because I warn you, we tax geeks are well-connected. For some strange reason, women find us irresistible. Maybe it's the way we make the IRS code sound dirty," he joked. "In fact, one of my clients is related to a big-time Hollywood agent, his brother or uncle. He might be willing to set me up."

"Sure, honey, you have my permission to date a big movie star."

Five weeks later, Katie and her friend Pamela were burrowed into a big couch in front of the television, slurping Pinot Gris while waiting for the Golden Globes to begin, their yearly girl's ritual. Robert always traveled to a legal convention this time of year. A cartoonish Melissa Rivers was hovering near the red carpet, harassing stars as they made their way into the building. Katie was filling her glass when Pamela shrieked.

"Katie, look! That guy with Penélope Cruz. He looks just like Robert. My God, it's…Katie, is that him? Is that Robert?"

Katie watched as her husband, one hand planted on the spot where Penélope's tiny waist blossomed into a curvy ass, stopped to converse with Rivers.

"Goooorgeous gown, Penélope. Just incredible," Melissa gushed. "God, I'd kill my firstborn for your body. Who are you wearing?"

"Stella McCartney," Penélope answered shyly.

"And your handsome date?" Rivers turned to Katie's husband.

"Robert," Penélope announced, wrapping her arm into his, and pushing her internationally acclaimed cleavage into his chest.

"Basic Armani." Robert smiled, hands spread wide to present the tuxedo Katie so clearly recognized.

"Gawd, what a gorgeous couple you two make," Rivers shrieked. "Get out of here and go make some babies. The world needs more good-looking people."

Katie watched Robert and Penélope Cruz turn and head into the theatre, suddenly realizing she didn't know her husband as well as she thought, regretting she hadn't opted for a new watch as his anniversary gift.

SECRET CREEK

YANCY HAD STUMBLED ACROSS the creek thirty years earlier. He and his wife Gracie had decided to introduce their new puppy to the forest, heading into the Gifford Pinchot wilderness for a Saturday afternoon drive. Rocky the lab emitted a hoarse bark that Yancy interpreted as pre-poop distress and quickly pulled to the side of the road, fine dust back rolling over his new Grand Cherokee. Rocky leapt from the Jeep and dashed into the bushes, Yancy on his heels yelling, "Rocky, no," followed by "Goddammit, Rocky" as the dog escaped farther into the brush.

Fifteen minutes later, shirt shredded by blackberry brambles, hands and knees caked with mud after stumbling over gnarled tree roots, Yancy discovered Rocky lapping from the most beautiful little creek he had ever seen. His anger dissipated when he saw the gin-clear water winding through a meadow and stand of firs and cedar trees, light filtering through hanging moss, like a magical brook from a fairy tale.

He'd been hiking this area for years and had no idea there was a stream hidden in this forest. He leashed Rocky and walked the bank. That's when he saw the fish. Water wound around a bend and flowed into a deep pool flanked by a high bank rimmed with river rock. There was movement under the surface, water dimpling as fish sipped flies off the surface. Yancy assumed they were finger-long cutthroats or steelhead smolt, the main population in these waters. Much to his dismay as a fly fisherman, the sparse trout population in this area tended to consist of fish too small to be sporting. He'd never figured out why Western Washington could birth massive salmonids but rarely produced a respectable trout, forcing him to make the pilgrimage to Montana or Idaho if he wanted to catch a serious brown or rainbow.

One of the feeding fish broke water, and Yancy gasped. It appeared to be a brown trout almost two feet long. *Impossible*, Yancy muttered. The closest brown trout were two hundred miles away. He couldn't imagine a fish that size lived in this small creek. *Must be a big whitefish. Maybe a wayward salmon.* He climbed to a higher bank for a better view.

Five large browns, all between twenty and twenty-eight inches long, circled the pool, darting up to slurp mayflies off the surface. He watched them for several more minutes until he heard Gracie's hollering through the trees.

This might be it, he thought to himself as he grabbed Rocky and navigated toward his wife's voice. Every angler dreamt of discovering secret water, a perfect undiscovered river chock full of trout.

~

THAT NIGHT HE SCOURED forest service maps trying to find the waterway, but according to every source he consulted, it did not exist. Must be an offshoot of one of the bigger rivers in the area, perhaps a tributary of the Wind or Paradise Creek, he figured.

At 9:00 p.m., he called his best friend, Martin. "Get packed up; we're going fishing tomorrow. I'll pick you up at six."

"Thanks," Martin said, "but no can do. I promised my folks we'd take them to mass."

"Screw mass. I promise you a much more impactful religious experience."

Yancy told Martin about the secret water.

"Are you drunk? Maybe whiffed a little glue by accident?" Martin asked. They had often discussed the secret water concept, assuming it was only a fantasy.

"I'm sober. It's real. I'm going to take you there."

"Well, Jesus was a fisherman, so I expect he'll understand," Martin said. "See you tomorrow."

The next morning, they pulled into the spot where Yancy had parked the previous day, and armed with their fly rods, they hiked through the difficult terrain to the stream.

"Holy shit," Martin said when he saw the water. "My apologies for inferring you were a glue-sniffing drunk."

Yancy nodded. "Wait until you see what lives here."

They approached the pool where he had seen the feeding fish. Yancy cautiously tossed a Parachute Adams into the riffle that poured into the deep hole. He watched the fly wind its way into the center, concerned that the fish he saw the day before might have been a mirage, then stiffened as a dark form emerged from the depths, fighting the temptation to set the hook as a huge trout nosed the bug, then shot back down under a rock. *A refusal.* The fly floated another two feet, and another fish darted out and slammed the Adams. Yancy raised his rod, firmly hooking the brown, which leapt three feet in the air.

Martin yelled, "Got him," as Yancy stepped backward and stripped in line to stay tight to the fish. "Jesus," Martin said. "That's a monster. Must be six or seven pounds."

The trout raced upstream, Yancy's reel screaming as the line stripped off. The fish went airborne again, then reversed course, now going deep. Yancy frantically tried to pull in line as the brown raced toward him. He knew a trout this size could easily break the tippet if he was too aggressive or throw the fly if he didn't stay firm. The brown shook and rumbled, and once it was to the reel, careened downstream. Yancy watched his reel spool into the backing, then began running after the fish to stay tight. He had sprinted fifty feet when the trout jumped again, jiggled ferociously, and snapped the line in mid-air. He dropped to his knees as Martin moaned.

Yancy shook his head, then started to laugh. "Did you see that?"

Martin nodded. "Where in the hell are we?"

"I told you we'd have a religious experience. I think this is Heaven." Yancy rose and slapped his friend on the back.

"I'm going to assume I'm still asleep," Martin said, "and this is just a magnificent dream, though it would be really perfect if I was fishing with Julia Roberts instead of you."

"Well, maybe she's around the next bend," Yancy said. "This place is full of surprises."

For the next eight hours, the two men explored the creek. The fish were so big they lost most they hooked but managed to land five huge, healthy trout that they examined and then gingerly released.

"We found our secret water," Yancy announced as they crawled back into his Jeep.

"I don't understand it," Martin said. "There shouldn't be brown trout here, especially that size. Where does the water come from, and how did those fish get here and grow so big?"

"Someone must have planted them a long time ago, and for some reason, they're doing well," Yancy theorized. "Maybe there's a special food source in the water; freshwater shrimp or big crawdads. Or they're a mutant strain of giant browns. Sea runs brought in from Iceland, something like that. I've never seen browns jump before; that's a rainbow trait. I can tell you one thing. We need to keep this a secret. If people knew about this place, it would be overrun and ruined. It needs to stay between you and me."

Martin reached into a cooler behind the seat to grab two beers. He popped the tops, handed one to his friend, and they clinked cans in a toast. "Here's to secret water," he said. "I promise I will never tell a soul about this place."

"To our secret," Yancy pledged.

Initially, they worried the fishing was a fluke; spawning browns temporarily moving through the waterway. However, every time they fished it was an adventure, huge trout taking tiny flies and grasshopper patterns, often breaking a ten-pound test line.

They ordered custom rods from C. F. Burkheimer to fish the water, short seven weights designed to handle large trout in a small stream.

Whenever they arrived at the creek, there was a moment of panic that they might spot another angler. They would carefully examine the mud and sand around the water for footprints but only found signs of deer and elk, and an occasional coyote.

They assigned names to their favorite pools and stretches of water, Martin favoring dead rock musicians: Big Bopper Pool, Jim Morrison Run, Elvis's Corner. Yancy stuck to the classics: Browntown, Hopper City, and Broken Rod.

For the next three decades, the men made the pilgrimage to Secret Creek, as they called it, twice a month. They fought the temptation to go more often but decided it best to rest the fish and minimize their impact on the water, protecting the place like their own temple. They never spoke of it to anyone, gingerly released everything they caught, and never photographed a fish, lest someone inquire where such monsters lived. Instead of parking by their trail, they would drive to a camping site a half mile past the turnout so nobody became curious about why they were parked on the road. They'd walk back and duck into the trees to avoid cars, even brushing away their footprints where they entered the woods.

When the internet bloomed, they ridiculed fishing buddies who broadcast their adventures with photos of large fish, happily identifying where they had caught the trout. "I want you to promise to shoot me in the head if I ever put up a Facebook or Instagram post of Secret Creek," Martin joked to Yancy, "because it means I'm senile, and it's time for me to go."

"You won't need to ask twice. In fact, the minute I sense you're even a bit off, I'll be happy to arrange a Dick Cheney," Yancy assured him.

One day, Martin called Yancy over to the bank on Broken Rod. "What do you make of this?" He pointed at the tracks: thick claws marked deep in mud.

"I'm no expert, but it looks like a wolf. They've been saying it's only a matter of time until they migrate this far west."

"You think we should be concerned?"

"Concerned about a bloodthirsty animal with razor-sharp teeth that could rip your throat out? A beast that kills just for the fun of it?" Yancy smiled. "Why? Would that dissuade you from coming here?" He gestured at the water.

"Fair point," Martin said. "I think I'll just assume it was a sweet little puppy dog with big paws that wandered through. Bingo was his name-o."

A month later, they met Bingo in person. They had rounded Hopper City when a massive gray wolf appeared eighty yards away, slowly emerging from a shadowy cove of hemlocks. He regarded them with yellow eyes, more curious than predatory.

"Jesus," Martin whispered. "What do we do?"

"Don't panic," Yancy said. "Keep an eye on him, and slowly back up."

The wolf seemed unconcerned. He watched them retreat, then ambled to the creek to lap water. Once they were out of sight, the men hustled back to the Jeep.

"Whew, gotta tell you, I almost shit my pants on that one," Martin said with relief.

"Almost?" Yancy asked, sniffing the air. "You mean this is how you normally smell?"

"Hey, that's the musky aroma of manhood. I was more afraid for you than me," Martin said. "I'm faster. I can't tell you how sad I would be at your funeral. It wouldn't be nearly as much fun fishing alone."

"That's what makes you such a great friend. Always concerned about my welfare," Yancy said. "Are we going to keep fishing Secret Creek, or will we let Bingo the big, bad wolf scare us away?"

Martin hesitated to think. "I think there's plenty of room for three of us on that water. Plus, as long as I can outrun you, I'm not too concerned."

After that, they would sometimes see Bingo in the distance, patrolling the edge of the forest, watching warily but never showing any sign of aggression. After a few months, they lost their fear, and the animal became another fascinating aspect of a place they couldn't believe existed.

YANCY HAD THREE LOVES in his life: his wife, Gracie; his daughter, Kathleen; and Secret Creek. If he wasn't feeling hypermasculine, he might even list Martin among the group, as they had been friends since they were five years old, and Martin was Kathleen's Godfather. Gracie and Kathleen knew about Secret Creek, but he had sworn them to secrecy even though both assured him that they and their friends had absolutely no interest in his fishing location.

"Daddy, let me know if you run across a secret spa in the forest run by hot leprechauns, and then we'll talk," his daughter joked.

One day Kathleen called from her home in Seattle to inform her parents she had met the man of her dreams and wanted to bring her new fiancé to Portland to meet them. Yancy and Gracie were thrilled. Yancy was hoping for a grandchild someday. Secret Creek would need to be bequeathed to someone when he and Martin were too old for the journey.

But when Kathleen and her boyfriend arrived, Yancy's creep alert went off. It started with the guy's name, Quinton Bellows. You don't get to choose your legal name, he theorized, but a real man named Quinton would shorten it to Quint, or even Q—as heinous as that currently sounded—just like any sane individual would shorten Charles to Charlie or Chuck. Bellows brought to mind the smarmy Major Bellows he used to watch as a kid on reruns of *I Dream of Jeannie*.

Yancy also believed you could judge a man by the way they interacted with animals. When Quinton entered the living room, the dog circled his legs for the perfunctory sniff test. Quinton tensed up, hands raised as if he were expecting an attack.

"Don't worry about Apollo," Kathleen said. "He's really friendly. Just wants to get to know you."

The dog finished his inspection, gave a disinterested snort, and returned to his bed.

Relieved the dog was retreating, Quinton delivered a forced laugh and relaxed. "Cute dog. Apollo. You're a fan of Greek gods?" he said to Yancy.

"No, he's a fan of Labs and Rocky movies," Kathleen said. "His first yellow lab was named Rocky. The second was Balboa. And this one was named after Apollo Creed."

Quinton worked in private equity, which Yancy regarded as a profession primarily populated with tax-dodging bottom-feeders and reprobates too lazy to find real work. He was a bit too coiffed for Yancy's taste, his hair slicked back like a helmet and his skinny slacks tugging at his groin, his shirt pressed so severely the creases looked hazardous.

And the guy was wearing jewelry! Quinton was adorned with bracelets, with three silver bands encircling his skinny fingers. The largest of the bracelets, a clump of silver ingots strung with a leather band, looked heavy enough to throw off his balance. When he was in high school, Yancy's class ring had gotten wedged in a gate, and he'd almost ripped his finger off. Real men fix stuff, and jewelry easily gets caught in the stuff they're fixing.

As they shook, Yancy noticed Quinton's soft hands and tangy cologne. Yancy hadn't worn cologne since 1977, when his high school girlfriend gave him a bottle of Aramis for Christmas. Yancy attempted to keep his conservative nature in check. He knew millennial men tended to be more metrosexual than his generation, but Quinton was a bit precious for his taste.

Yancy had always secretly hoped for a son-in-law who might appreciate knocking around the woods with him. Someone that would enjoy a Blazers game followed by a stop at Rusty's for a beer and a game of pool. A guy who owned a shotgun and knew how to change a tire. Quinton looked like the kind of man who ironed his sheets.

He was kind enough to bring a bottle of wine, but as he presented it to Gracie, Quinton delivered a two-minute soliloquy on the incredible heritage of the grapes, including crass references to the cost. "A lot of people might think a wine like this is a bit indulgent," he said with a fox's grin, "but it's been a very good year for me, and I figured only the best for Kathleen's parents." Yancy knew his way around a cellar and mentally noted it was a vintage purchased by people anxious to impress but with little knowledge of oenology.

Quinton spent the two-hour dinner pontificating about the enormous societal benefit he and his financial brethren were bestowing on lowly business owners. "I'm in the business of making the common man rich," he said proudly. "These companies are like rough clay that I help hone into something beautiful." Yancy felt inclined to wade in with an alternative opinion that contained words like "parasite" and "leech," but Kathleen looked so happy he fought his temptation to confront the blowhole.

"Daddy, you two have something in common," she announced.

Yancy could not imagine what that could possibly be but tried to lighten his own grumpy demeanor. "Quint's a fan of classic rock and roll? You like Bachman-Turner Overdrive and The Doobie Brothers?"

Quinton winced at having his name shortened. He had been careful to correct Yancy earlier in the conversation, clarifying he went by Quinton and not Quint.

"No, Dad, you're the only one in the world that likes those bands. Quinton loves to fly fish."

Yancy had a hard time imagining this guy wading a river. "Really? Where do you fish?"

"I'm a bit new to the sport," Quinton said. "I learned a couple of years ago when I was at a meeting in Jackson Hole, and I loved it. The guide said I was a natural. Said my cast looked like I'd been doing it all my life."

Yancy fought the urge to wretch.

"Since then, I've become a fanatic. If I could, I'd spend all my time standing by a river with my pole."

"Rod," Yancy said.

"What?" Quinton looked confused.

"A fly fisherman uses a rod, not a pole. And you usually stand in the river. A pole with a worm is what you use to catch catfish down at the old fishing hole," he quipped, "when you and Huck skip school."

"Dad, I was telling Quinton about your secret spot with the huge fish," Kathleen interrupted. "I thought you could take him out there this weekend."

Yancy froze. "You told him about Secret Creek?"

"Daddy, Quinton's going to be family. There are no secrets in the family."

"I've really been looking forward to it," Quinton said. "Kathleen said it's incredible. I even brought my gear. I have a new Orvis..." he stopped and smiled, "...rod."

"Excuse me a second." Yancy felt dizzy and retreated into the kitchen. Gracie followed him.

"Stop it," she said.

"Stop what?"

"Stop being a jerk to your daughter's fiancé. I know it seems like he's not your kind of guy, but you need to get to know him. Kathleen's a smart girl, and if she loves him, he must be special."

"Secret Creek is a secret," he said. "Hence the name. You know that. For thirty years, Martin and I have never told a soul about it, and now she invites some kid I've never even met."

"Well, maybe it's high time someone else gets to enjoy your private stream," Gracie said. "And it would be a good opportunity for the two of you to bond. I'm sure your daughter wants you to love him too. Take him tomorrow. It will give me a chance to spend some time with Kathleen. We have a wedding to plan."

Yancy knew better than to argue. He slumped into his den to call Martin and give him the news. "Jesus," Martin said. "I can't believe you broke the promise."

~

THE NEXT DAY ON the drive to Secret Creek, both men instructed Quinton on the rules. "You can never tell anyone about this place. Never." Yancy barked. "And please don't ever come here unless you're with us."

"No pictures. We don't want anyone to see it," Martin added. "We're really careful with the fish. Barbless hooks, always catch and release, and make sure they're healthy before you let them go."

"Got it," Quinton said. "But I gotta say, you guys are a bit paranoid about your fishing spot."

Yancy and Martin helped Quinton navigate the brush, as he tripped over tree roots, whining loudly. Once they reached the stream, he perked up and quickly demonstrated his complete lack of expertise with a fly rod. He slapped at the water, sending the trout skittering. "Damn wind," he said in frustration as his casts snagged in the brush, even though it was a calm day. Martin had more patience than Yancy and coached him until he finally hooked a fish on Browntown. The trout ran hard downstream, spooling Quinton before it finally broke off when he allowed the line to wrap around the reel.

"Damn cheap reel," he screamed, as he threw the rod to the ground.

"Didn't have anything to do with the reel," Martin said calmly. "You need to keep the line in control."

"That was a big fish," Quinton said, regaining his composure. "You guys were right about this place. I've never hooked anything like that."

Quinton lost several more trout before finally landing one a few minutes before they returned to the Jeep, and for the first ten minutes of the drive home, he regaled the men with detailed descriptions of every trout he had hooked that day, as if they had not been there.

"We have a fishing rule," Yancy finally said. "We only talk about the fish we catch, not the ones we didn't."

Quinton ignored the comment. "Secret Creek is incredible. I can't believe you guys don't go there every day."

"Let's recap Secret Creek rules," Martin said. "We don't tell anyone about it. We are considerate of the water and only come twice a month. We carefully release the fish and use barbless hooks. We never take pictures, and we only come here together. Fair enough?"

"Sure. Absolutely." Quinton agreed. "Happy you guys included me. It will be our secret."

Yancy glanced at Martin. They had agreed to take a convoluted route in the hope that Quinton would be unable to find his way back.

A wedding date was set for the following summer. While Yancy was not happy about the marriage, he was thrilled that Kathleen was spending more weekends in Portland, planning the event with Gracie. At first, Quinton accompanied her, which dampened Yancy's enthusiasm, sometimes necessitating he take him to Secret Creek, but after a couple of trips Quinton stayed in Seattle.

Three months before the wedding, Kathleen showed up unexpectedly. She was distraught and informed her parents that she had called off the wedding. "We had a big fight." She told them. "It turns out that when I was coming to Portland, he was seeing an old girlfriend. And get this…she's pregnant."

"Oh, Kathleen, I'm so sorry." Gracie moved forward to comfort her daughter.

Kathleen held up a hand. "It gets worse. I caught him lying about all kinds of things. He isn't a partner at the firm. He was just an executive assistant, and he was fired three months ago. He's been acting like he was going off to work when he isn't even working. I was an idiot. He borrowed money from me, claiming it was for the big secret honeymoon he was planning. Six thousand dollars!

He said all his cash was tied up in a huge deal that was going to pay off right after the wedding. *We'll be rich*, he kept saying, but he was living off my cash. That fancy fly rod he bought to impress you..." she pointed at Yancy, "he charged it to my credit card." Kathleen paced the room, growing angrier. "You know how he was always bragging about Stanford? He didn't even graduate from college. He flunked out of San Francisco State."

Yancy was not surprised—and secretly rejoiced—but did his best to comfort his daughter. "The guy's a sociopath," he said. "They're good at deceiving people because they believe their own bullshit. You're lucky you found out now."

The next morning, she came down to breakfast, looking pale and even more rattled. "Dad, I have to show you something." She handed him her phone. "I'm so sorry. I can't believe he would do this. He put this up yesterday. He just wanted to get back at me."

The screen was open to a Facebook post on Quinton's page. There were several pictures of Secret Creek. When they weren't looking, he'd managed to take photos, including a few of fish. He had also secretly pinned the coordinates and posted a map. BIGGEST BROWN TROUT YOU'VE EVER SEEN, the headline screamed. BE THERE SATURDAY.

Yancy stared at the images. "I'm going to kill him," he muttered.

"Maybe nobody will pay any attention to it," Kathleen tried to comfort him. "He doesn't have many friends."

Yancy called Martin to give him the bad news, and twenty minutes later, Martin pulled up in front of the house. Gracie and Kathleen trailed Yancy to Martin's pickup, pleading with them not to go. "Nothing good can come of this," Gracie said. "The damage is done. He wants you to be upset. Don't give him the satisfaction."

"Just have to see how badly he's screwed it up," Yancy said.

"Well, for God's sake, don't hurt him," Gracie said. "I don't want you going to prison."

"I won't touch him," Yancy said, then added quietly, "but he might," motioning at Martin. After a few minutes of silence in the truck, Yancy finally spoke. "I'm really sorry about this. It's all my fault."

"True," Martin said. "I guess you didn't understand the concept of a secret. But don't sweat it. I wouldn't want you to feel bad about the fact that you ruined one of the best parts of our lives. Or that you broke a pledge we've had for thirty years. I'm sure we can find another secret creek full of huge trout for you to blab about."

Yancy sighed and dropped his head, and Martin realized how bad his friend was feeling.

"Hell, Yance, really…it's okay. If it's ruined, well, we were lucky enough to have all these years of great fishing. You were kind enough to show it to me, which I will always appreciate. We might even get to have a little fun today. Kick his lying ass around the forest."

They arrived at the cutoff to discover three SUVs parked alongside the road. There was a yellow flag hanging from a tree, indicating where the trail began. Yancy moaned when he saw that someone had taken a machete and hacked a clearing.

"Jesus Christ," Martin yelled fifty yards into the woods when they came across discarded beer cans and potato chip wrappers littering the ground. He bent to pick up the trash.

When they emerged from the brush near the stream, two men carrying rods were walking toward them. "Hope you aren't here to fish," one of them said as they passed Martin and Yancy, heading back to the road. "It was a hoax. Goddamn Quinton wasted our weekend."

Yancy and Martin threw each other confused glances, but when they reached the stream, they understood. Secret Creek was gone, replaced by a muddy trickle of water circulating through a weed-infested field. The pool that had held huge fish was now an outcrop of Scotch broom, and downed logs blocked what used to be a long, deep stretch.

"Are we in the wrong spot?" Martin asked. "Maybe came out of the trail too soon."

"Thirty years we've been coming here. We're in the right place. Look at the rock bank. This is Elvis's Corner."

"But…" Martin paced up and down where the creek had been. "How could this happen? We were here two weeks ago. It looks like it's been this way for years. Where's the water?"

"Maybe it got dammed upstream," Yancy said.

"But that wouldn't make it look like this. Look at all the vegetation. Those trees. That couldn't happen in two weeks."

Two more fishermen approached. "Hey, do you guys know where we can find the stream? We've walked all over the place."

Yancy shook his head. "It was a hoax. Another of Quinton's lies."

The bigger of the two men flashed red. "Why in the hell would he do that? We drove over a hundred miles."

"He likes to screw with people," Martin said. "He wanted to see how many idiots would come out."

The man flexed forward. Martin was six foot one, and the man was a head taller and thirty years younger. "Are you calling me an idiot?"

"No, no," Martin held up his hands. "Quinton's words, not mine. He lied to us too."

"Quinton's going to regret his little joke," the man said as he strode off.

"Not a guy I'd want upset with me," Yancy said.

"But I would like to be there when he finds Quinton," Martin answered, then looked back at the remnants of Secret Creek. "What the hell is going on?"

Yancy and Martin walked a mile upstream but could find no sign of the creek, just an occasional muddy bog. "You know, sometimes when we were here, I couldn't believe the place existed. It was like something we dreamed up," Yancy said.

"You think we were just hallucinating the hundreds of times we fished?" Martin motioned around them. "Maybe those trees are magical. Throw off a little psilocybin fairy dust that got us high?"

"You got a better explanation?"

When they emerged from the forest, there was only one SUV parked on the road. Yancy recognized it as Quinton's. "The asshole is still back there somewhere," Yancy pointed at the vehicle.

"Maybe the big guy found him and delivered a beating," Martin said.

"Let's hope."

When Yancy got home and tried to explain the situation to Gracie and Kathleen, he realized he sounded insane.

"Dad, I know you're just trying to make me feel better with your crazy story. You don't need to do that. I'm so sorry," Kathleen said.

Yancy decided it was best never to discuss Secret Creek with anyone but Martin.

Kathleen returned to Seattle feeling better after a calming weekend with her parents and friends but called her mother and father the next Saturday with new stress. "Quinton's missing."

"What do you mean?"

"I had a call from a detective. He wanted to know if I had talked to him. Nobody has heard from him in almost a week. His parents are going crazy. He never returned from Secret Creek. They found his car parked on the road, and his cell phone was sitting in some bushes. They have a search party combing the area. Daddy," she hesitated. "You didn't..."

"Didn't what?" Yancy said.

"Well, it's just that you told us that nutty story, and I was worried that maybe you were covering up the fact that you found Quinton, and something happened?"

"You think I killed your fiancé and buried him in the woods?"

"Ex-fiancé," she blurted. "No, it's just that I know how much you loved that place. And if you ran into him, well, I could see how things could get out of hand. If something did happen, you could tell us. Of course, I didn't say anything to the detective about how Quinton found Secret Creek. There's no connection to you."

"Well, thanks for not implicating me in a murder. Jesus, Kathleen, I can't believe you think your dad's a killer. We saw Quinton's car, but we didn't see him. And there were guys there even more upset with him than me. Anything could have happened."

"Okay, Dad, I just wanted you to know what was going on."

The next day Yancy and Martin returned to Secret Creek. There were several forest service and sheriff's vehicles and a Skamania County Search and Rescue van parked alongside the road. A few men were milling about, and they stopped and approached the group.

"Did you find him?" Yancy asked.

"Nope," one of the men replied. He looked exhausted and stubbed a cigarette out on the ground before taking a swig from a water bottle. "Not a sign. We've covered every inch for five square miles."

Yancy involuntarily winced when he saw the condition of the trail. With all the traffic, a six-foot-wide swath had been cleaved through the brush.

"Did you find a creek?" Yancy asked.

"No creek, but a lot of mud. It's tough terrain. Not sure why this guy would even go in there," the man said.

"Strange situation," Martin said as they got back in the truck.

"Sure is. My family thinks I'm either insane or a murderer. And I wonder a bit about my own sanity."

"That's wise. I've often doubted your mental acuity. But it's a stretch to call you insane. I know for a fact you didn't murder the kid."

"Thanks for your support." Yancy smiled, then turned serious. "Martin, it was real, wasn't it?"

"Well, you know what they say," Martin said. "We all just exist in a dog's dream. Maybe the pooch got bored with Secret Creek."

~

A YEAR LATER, KATHLEEN called to let her parents know that Quinton had been declared legally dead. "They never found a sign of him," she said. "His parents blame me for breaking up with him.

They think he might have committed suicide. They don't know their son very well. I think he took off. Couldn't take the pressure. No job, a pregnant girlfriend, our breakup. He's probably on some beach in Cabo scamming tourists."

"Nice to hear you're taking it so well," Yancy said. "And I'm happy you decided I'm not a killer."

THE FOLLOWING SPRING, YANCY and Martin were driving to Rusty's for a Saturday afternoon beer and a game of pool. "A year ago, we were fishing Secret Creek," Martin said longingly.

"Aren't you curious?"

"Course I am, but I've been afraid to go back. I'm spooked by the whole thing. Not sure if we're nuts, or there's some kind of magic we can't possibly comprehend."

"We need to know."

Martin nodded, then veered toward the freeway. Ninety minutes later, they parked by the entrance to Secret Creek. The forest had reclaimed the pathway, wild blackberry brambles and scrub maple covering the entrance. They fought their way through the thicket and emerged into the clearing. Their beautiful little river was back, shiny water cascading out of the forest. They walked to Elvis's Pool and watched brown trout dart in and out of rocks, rising to slurp flies.

Neither man spoke. They paced the bank, marveling at the water. Yancy finally turned to look at Martin, who shrugged with an "I have absolutely no idea" motion. When they reached Jim Morrison Run, they were startled to see Bingo amble out of the trees fifty feet away, trailed by a young wolf about half Bingo's size. They froze in place. "Looks like Bingo found a friend," Martin said nervously. "Or that's Bingo Jr."

This was the closest they had ever come, but the wolves seemed calm. Bingo Jr. moved closer, clamping something in his teeth. He slowly stepped another five feet, then dropped it on the sandy bank, turned around, and the two trotted back into the trees.

They walked forward, Yancy falling to one knee to pick up what the wolf had left behind. He cleaned off the dirt and immediately recognized the bracelet: lumps of silver threaded with a strip of leather. *Heavy*, he thought, picturing it on Quinton's wrist. *I could have told him wearing jewelry was dangerous.* The bracelet felt hot, like it might singe his hand, and he flung it into a deep pool as if it were infecting him. They watched it sink, until sand and rocks and bright green plants lining the bottom of the stream reclaimed it. There was a tiny flash as sunlight hit an ingot, and a thick trout appeared to nudge the shiny object, sending up a swirl of dirt that settled and made it disappear forever.

THE KLANSMAN

I'VE SPENT FIFTY-ONE YEARS dodging questions about my daddy. Those who spawn from normal origins don't appreciate the satisfaction of being able to say, "My father's an accountant or plumber."

I'd just rejoice at being the son of an honest man.

If you're not of the Anglo-Saxon persuasion, people expect—even appreciate—a response that fits their sociological perspective: *Dad's in prison. Dad abandoned us. I never knew my dad.* Those all sound right to white folks when discussing the family lineage of people of color; it's convenient to forget that the trailer park is a Caucasian concept. In my case, any one of those answers would be better than my truth. How does a black man explain he was fathered by an evil racist cracker?

Nice to meet you. My Pop? He's a fat, white piece of rapist shit that rose through the Klan, then celebrated his retirement by chaining the doors shut on an African American church and torching it up with kerosene and hay bales.

Maybe you heard of him, Clayton Lucius Bowers. Fancy southern name that translates to psychotic redneck. Killed nine people, including two old ladies and three kids he fried right in front of Jesus and Mary. And that doesn't count the men he lynched when he was young, maybe to earn one of those fancy merit badges that dressed up his white robe.

There's a family tale that would liven up a dinner party. Course, it's a story I'll never tell.

Truth is, I never knew the man existed until I was twenty years old. When I was growing up, Ma's tall tale regarding my conception was that she'd had an impulsive fling with a boy just passing through—a sweet send-off before he shipped out to Vietnam—where he promptly got his ass blown up. I grew up thinking she'd donated her cherry to the war effort, and I was the product of that patriotic coupling. "Pop was killed in Vietnam," sounded a lot better than the excuses some of my friends had for skipping dad and lad functions. I'd have never known the truth, till my mom decided to tell me for my own protection.

At the time, I was beginning to be somebody. By the late 1970s, hip-hop was on the move. What began as Bronx street music was suddenly selling in record stores—white kids in Wisconsin and Arizona suddenly grooving—much to their parents' horror, to scary-looking brothers scraping turntables. From our little apartment in Bedford Park, I was front row. While the smart kids were studying math and science, I pursued my own degree in urban musicality, analyzing The Sugarhill Gang, Grandmaster Flash, and The Fat Boys. The men that would define an entirely new sound were roaming my neighborhood figuring it out, and I was there. My big break came when I opened for Run-DMC in 1983.

At that point, Ma came to me. "Something you need to know," she said. "Something I lied about all these years." Just that sentence was shocking, for as far as I knew, Ma invented the "straight and narrow."

Despite the fact that Sarah had lived the most virtuous existence possible, she'd always struggled. All she had was our tiny apartment in Brooklyn, and a son that preferred music and weed to honest employment. She'd worked her butt off for the last two decades cleaning rooms at a sad-looking Marriott. On Sunday, she'd donate her time to the church, helping people that often weren't as poor as us. And she spent her free time making sure I was respectable, never afraid to use a belt to slap some goodness into me.

"I got to tell you something I'd hoped I never had to admit, but as famous as you gettin', somebody might dig it up," she said. "When I was growing up in Arkansas, my mother cleaned house for the Bowers family. I'd stop by after school to help out. They were a hateful group," she whispered. "Deep Klan roots goin' back generations. One afternoon, when I was fourteen, the Bowers boy, Clayton Lucius, dragged me into the barn. Had his way with me. He was no kid, probably twenty-five at the time. I tried to get away, but he was a big fat thing, and I was no match. Laid his smelly body on me till I could barely breathe. Stunk of dirty shoes and Ripple. Told me if I ever mentioned it, he and the Klan would kill my whole family. Do to my mother and sisters what he did to me. Those days there was no law to protect against people like that."

When it became clear she was carrying me, Ma ran away to New York to live with an aunt. That's where I was born; it was fortunate I favored my mother's side of the family, with skin like chocolate milk, so you'd never know I was part white devil. She didn't want Clayton or any of the Bowers to know I existed.

Clayton Lucius had other problems. Between the Kennedys, Doctor King, and that redneck Lyndon Johnson, the hammer was falling. He'd spent his life pursuing his dream of being a big man in the Klan, but by the time he became Grand Wizard, men in white robes had denigrated from being feared to ridiculed. All of a sudden, we had famous black actors and politicians. A Negro and a white woman could walk down the street together holding hands—as long as they weren't in Alabama—and Clayton Lucius became a "Boss Hawg" parody.

I suspect that seeing his whole world come down was too much for him. So, he went and earned himself a place in the history books. In 1974, belly full of beer and who-knows-what, he chained up the doors during evening service at the Grace Baptist Church, then torched the place. He was stupid enough to brag, assuming his kind of hate was still widespread, and they caught him within a few days.

It was big news, and they were quick to make an example of him, sentencing Clayton Lucius to execution. Somehow, the porky bastard managed to avoid his final sentence. He's been on death row in a lovely institution called the Varner Supermax, which isn't nearly as nice as it sounds. I tried to put the man out of my mind, the way a person attempts to forget they carry the herpes virus. You pretend it isn't there, until it swells up and you can't avoid it.

And I was busy with my career. Thirty years of playing bigger and bigger venues, with a Grammy to put on the shelf every few years. A couple marriages and divorces. The good one that stuck bore two fabulous children. Once I hit fifty, I settled into the laid-back life of dad and legendary music producer, spending most of my time in the little studio in the back of my Long Island estate, or shooting hoops with the kids. We wanted Ma to move in with us, but she preferred to stay with her friends and little church, so I bought her a nice townhouse in the old neighborhood, bringing her out to play grandma most weekends.

Then one day, our angry old virus flares-up. Mom calls and shocks me by saying, "I think it's time you meet your sad excuse for a daddy. Get a peek before the fat bastard passes on to hell. Word is, he's close. Payback for all that sinning and fried food. He's got the diabetes so bad they chopped off his feet."

I argued, perplexed as to why she had any interest in reliving that event. But when Sarah's made up her mind, you might as well just go along. And I must admit I was curious.

It took a few weeks for my lawyers to work out the visit; officials wondered why a black celebrity and his elderly mom wanted to visit a notorious killer. We inferred that I was producing a documentary on racism, which also might feature an interview with the warden. The prospect of fame opens a lot of doors.

I picked up Ma, and we headed to Teterboro to catch my jet. She likes to complain about what a silly waste it is to fly private, but once she settles into that oversized leather seat, and the flight attendant brings her a Bloody Mary *(Just one, mind you.)*, she wears a big grin.

As usual, she pulled out her knitting. The woman is obsessed with yarn, and whenever she's visiting, I have to rush the kids upstairs to put on one of the sweaters she's always making for them. On my last trip to Italy, I'd bought her collapsible knitting needles made from exotic bone and a sack full of merino that cost more than three Armani turtlenecks. "I'm making you a fine hat," she announced happily. "Soft as a baby's rear to keep your big elephant ears warm."

"Ma, I still don't understand why we're doing this." I said. "Why in the world would you want to see him? What good could come of it?"

"A man going to his grave, especially a bad man, deserves to know the whole truth about his life," she answered. "I want Clayton to see the one fine thing he helped produce—you."

"Somehow, I doubt that he's going to be happy about having a son with my complexion," I said. "I don't understand why you would feel the least bit charitable toward the asshole."

"Watch your language," she said, throwing her icicle stare.

JUST IN CASE YOU'RE planning a little tour of Arkansas, I wouldn't put the Varner Supermax on the "must-visit" list. Aside from a few medieval dungeons I've toured in Europe, I've never seen a piece of architecture that felt more like death and misery.

But the warden gave us a warm greeting, and I spent the first few minutes signing autographs and posing for pictures. There didn't seem to be any security concerns surrounding our visit. Nobody patted us down.

"Not sure how much you'll get out of old Clayton," the warden said. "He's in a wheelchair and pretty far gone. Whatever little brain he used to have might not operate anymore."

They set us up in the warden's conference room, and a few minutes later wheeled in my father, retreating out the door to give us privacy. I have to admit it was a shock to finally meet the man. I'd thought emotion might well up. A sense of recognition at a cellular level that would flood me with a reaction. But looking at Clayton, I had a hard time believing I could have sprung from his loins. Bald and pasty white, he was skinny, yet somehow obese, like he was melting from the inside. His legs ended in stubs, covered with tattered gray socks that came to a point.

He looked up at us with rheumy eyes. "Who the hell are you?" he asked in a gravelly Southern accent.

"Clayton, you don't look so good," Mom rose and leaned into him. "What's the matter? Don't recognize me?"

"I don't know you," he said.

"You don't remember?" Ma asked sarcastically. "You don't recall that afternoon when you dragged me into the barn and raped me? Put your filthy little thing in me?" She punctuated "filthy little thing" by poking him hard in the chest.

Clayton's eyes flashed. "Get the hell away from me. You crazy," he said. "I wouldn't touch your old black ass."

I was about to plant a fist in his face, but Ma rose a hand to keep me in my seat. "You probably don't remember because I was just a child. It happened over fifty years ago."

He hesitated, then threw a nasty grin, as if he'd found some new source of energy, and inspected Ma more closely. "Well, let's see. Fifty years? Maybe I do remember. You were a pretty young thing, as I recall. Big ole titties for your age. I recall we had a lot of fun." Then his face screwed up in hate. "A white man can't rape a colored girl. You should be thanking me for paying you a little attention." He gave a crazy little giggle. "Fact is, I used to have my way with a lot of your kind, so it's hard to keep you straight."

"Well, I do have one thing to thank you for," she said, pointing at me. "This fine gentleman you helped produce. Luckily, he doesn't take after you. He's a good soul. Rich and famous too. We flew out here in his private jet. I wanted you to meet your black son before you fall into hell."

Clayton frowned. "You crazy old bitch. There's no way I could father him. Someone pay you to come here and say that nonsense? One of those commie liberal groups always causing trouble for me?"

"No, Clayton. Meet your son. He's a successful black man with a fine family. Nothing like the filthy pedophile that fathered him," Mom said proudly.

The old man sneered and raised a wilted finger. "That goddamn monkey don't possess any of my blood, that's for sure. Maybe the truth is you just wanted to get in here so you could be near to me again. Is that what this is about? You miss old Clayton?"

Ma snorted.

"Well, you old and ugly now, but maybe just for old time's sake I'll give you another ride. My old dick could use a workout," Clayton said, feebly grabbing his crotch.

"Is that your dying wish?" Ma asked. "Do a little more evil?" She raised her right hand behind her back, and that's when I saw the knitting needle, clenched in her closed fist. "We won't be doing that, but I'd be happy to give you something to remember me by," she said, driving her arm forward.

Clayton screamed as the knitting needle pierced his thin pajama bottoms, blood staining below his waist. "Bitch," he howled.

Ma wiped the bloody needle on the leg of his pajamas before collapsing it and sticking it back in her purse. The door burst open, and a confused guard and the warden rushed in. "What happened?" the Warden asked.

"He got all worked up, and I think he had some kind of hemorrhage," Ma said with Oscar-worthy concern. "Appears something burst up inside him. You better get him to the hospital."

"Stabbed me in my dick," Clayton bellowed, which in his garbled tone sounded more like "stamped me in da duck."

"Get him to the infirmary," the warden directed the guard. Clayton kept screaming, but his words were nonsensical as they wheeled him down the hallway.

We moved back into the warden's office. "Jesus, what went on in here?" he asked.

"He wasn't making sense," I replied. "Said crazy things, like he was having some kind of breakdown. All of a sudden, he started clawing at himself, and the next thing you know, he's bleeding. Like Ma said, maybe some kind of hemorrhage."

The warden looked at me with suspicion.

"I'm sorry for any problems we've created," I continued. "He was in no shape to interview. You told us that. I hope this doesn't get you in trouble." The warden looked down, as if searching for what to do. "I want to make it up to you," I said. "How about this? Beyoncé is going to be performing in Little Rock next month. Why don't I get tickets for your family? I could arrange a little backstage tour. Bet your daughter would love to meet Beyoncé. I'll book a couple hotel suites so you can stay the night. Have a nice dinner; make it a real event."

The warden looked up in surprise, then smiled. "I expect she'd love that. And don't fret about Clayton. The man's been at death's door for a while."

We said our goodbyes and hurried out. I felt sure he'd keep a cap on the incident. The best way to a man's heart is to make him appear larger than life to his kids.

I didn't say anything to Ma until we were at 35,000 feet. "Jesus, is that why you had me bring you here? So you could attack the man? For all we know, you killed him."

She looked serene. "If you knew your bible, you'd know there's a fair bit of talk concerning an eye for an eye. Jesus understands that sometimes you need to give evil a hard slap."

"Well, you're full of surprises," I said, now smiling.

When she saw I wasn't upset, Ma smiled too. "Did you see Clayton Lucius's face? I think that needle went right through his little redneck pecker," laughing with fifty years of relief. "Son, tell that pretty girl to bring me another Bloody Mary," she said, motioning at the flight attendant. "I know it's past my limit, but I feel like celebrating."

PUBLIC SERVANT

I'm a liar. Always have been, always will be, though I might even be lying about that.

There are a wide variety of lucrative careers available to the accomplished prevaricator, and I experimented with several—finance, law, multi-level marketing—before choosing the most obvious and cliched profession for the truth-challenged. A very wise man, perhaps even me, once said, "People either go into politics to help other people or because they're too ugly to become actors." Ninety percent of politicians fall into the latter category. If I'd had George Clooney's looks, I am confident I could have lied my way to an Oscar, but instead, I worked my way through the political process to serve three terms in the United States Senate.

I discovered the power of dishonesty while growing up in Billings, Montana—which could now be best described as a Walmart surrounded by a moat of meth labs, but at the time was a bucolic little burg. My neighborhood was a gift to returning WWII vets: cracker boxes devoid of architectural charm but easy to own thanks to the GI bill, replete with healthy lawns, shag carpeting, and good public schools the greatest generation deemed essential. Fertile farms were plowed over to create this suburbia, but there were still remnants of a bygone agrarian era: a few tall farmhouses and barns overseeing an acre or two of corn and a few chickens surrounded by rows of identical 1,500 square-foot homes.

I was seven or eight years old when I told my first whopper. I promised my parents I would never play with matches, though at the time, my fascination with flame was much stronger than my concept of honesty, and besides, one of the few allures of growing up Catholic was the fact that any transgression was easily erased from your eternal record by five or six *Our Fathers*. I adored fire. The pang of sulfur wafting to your nostrils as flame erupted from a wooden kitchen match, the hot red and yellow of matter transformed into creamy ash. Like an addict seeking an even bigger high, I needed more than the thrill of tiny eruptions, or even the small bonfires I built in the alley.

An old barn that had survived the neighborhood development stood a block away. The ancient wood and an interior covered with dry straw was too strong a temptation for a firebug. It was not my intention to burn down the structure—I'm not an arsonist—I just wanted to see flames as tall as me. A child cannot comprehend the carnage of an out-of-control fire, and I was shocked and terrified when the blaze engulfed the entire building.

I escaped through an open door, terrified, and concerned that my actions might transform my neighborhood into charred heaps. I ran to the nearby farmhouse and banged loudly until an elderly woman opened the door and summoned help. Thanks to my prompt action, the fire department was there in a few minutes and extinguished the flames before they spread past the now-destroyed barn.

I explained to the firefighters and the old woman that I was walking by when I heard a loud pop emanating from the barn and saw three teenagers run out the back and across the field. "I think they were setting off fireworks," I postulated with disgust. "My parents won't let me play with fireworks unless I am with them," I added self-righteously. Since it was June 28, and the fireworks stands were open, this seemed logical, and the old woman and fire chief started heaping praise.

"Thank God you were here," the chief said, tousling my hair affectionately. The old woman hugged me, insisting I come in the house for milk and cookies. I was enjoying my newfound hero status so much that I decided to add more details to the incident, enthralling them with precise descriptions of the teenage criminals. The chief insisted on driving me home, congratulating my mother on raising such a fine child.

Much to my surprise, a few hours later, a reporter from the *Billings Gazette* stopped by to pen a story about the city's newest young hero, which also reflected well on my parents and teachers. Obviously, they were doing a great job to produce a child of such outstanding bravery and character.

And just like that, I was hooked. My little fabrication resulted in joy for many people, and thanks to my quick action, my neighborhood was saved! Of course, the old woman lost her barn, but it was a decrepit old structure she barely used, and the insurance money allowed her to remodel her bathroom, even adding one of those old-folk walk-in tubs advertised in the back of *Parade Magazine*. One downside: the police located three teenagers they accused of the crime, but I am sure they were hooligans that owed penance for other infractions, and besides, they never spent any time in jail. So, good for everyone involved.

Going forward, I was regarded as a golden child in my hometown, and I took great pains to maintain the facade. At the time, there was a popular book floating around called *How to Win Friends and Influence People*. I could synthesize that book into two words: kiss ass. False flattery is a wonderful form of lying that is good for everyone, and I was quick to master it.

Miss Edwards, my semiliterate spinster crone of a third-grade teacher, had probably never received anything resembling a compliment, so when I gazed at her adoringly and told her she was my favorite teacher, it created another win-win. I received a completely undeserved "A," and she went home thrilled that she had made the right career choice, even though a disproportionate percentage of her students ended up in careers requiring steel-toed boots.

I applied the same technique with my teachers all the way through law school. Combined with a talent for cheating on tests, and my ability to get much more knowledgeable friends to write my papers, I managed to stay near the top of my class academically. My instructors were thrilled to hone a developing mind that expressed so much approbation for them, and my co-conspirators were either financially compensated or heaped with the praise that helps a young person develop confidence in an otherwise difficult world.

This talent also allowed me to date women who normally would have had zero interest in a man of my mediocre appearance and doughy construction but who were susceptible to flattery and wit. Unfortunately, I am incapable of remaining faithful, and while my indiscretions were momentarily painful to some of the women I charmed, in the end, they were better off without me.

In the world of politics, a spouse is a highly desirable sign of stability, and I was lucky enough to discover a wonderful woman comfortable with living a deception. Sylvia is a hawk-faced heiress with a voracious appetite for plastic surgery and girls thirty years her junior. Given the terms of her prudish trust, she needed a beard, and I was the ideal solution. She spends most of her time in New York and Paris, entertaining bulimic waif-thin model wannabees seeking entry into her family's fashion empire. We occasionally meet to attend important galas or be photographed together while receiving awards or hobnobbing with the elite.

There is an old saying about plastic surgery, a particularly violent form of lying: the best surgery is the one you can't detect. This is true for all lies. Over the years, I made many rookie mistakes, spouting outrageous statements easily debunked. I once claimed at a party to have served as a Navy Seal, only to be questioned about my service by a retired admiral lurking nearby. To gain the favor of a beautiful young woman, I bragged about my expertise on the slopes, looking quite foolish a month later when she insisted we vacation in Aspen, where I was awarded a ride down the hill in a ski patrol sled.

Before I became famous, I used to tell people I had friendships with obscure celebrities. I don't know why I thought it impressive to lie that I had surfed with David Hasselhoff, appeared as an extra in two episodes of *Friends*, and spent a weekend in Cabo drinking with Nicolas Cage. I'm sure many people found it hard to imagine me working a short stint as a standup comedian in Los Angeles. During a round of "guy-talk," I floated the idea that as a young man, I had been intimate with a tipsy Sharon Stone, a statement I was prepared to extrapolate on but which was met with such ridicule that I realized it would be impossible to defend. And, of course, I quickly retired the celebrity tale involving "my good friend" Bill Cosby.

The best lies delight and amaze the listener while being difficult to contradict. The audience is rapt when I tell them about returning to my hotel room in Ochos Rios, Jamaica, only to encounter an armed intruder, or the time in Flagstaff when I was a brave bystander in a bank robbery. Faux friendships with dead people are generally safe territory. Given my political persuasion, my constituents are impressed to hear the advice Ronald Reagan gave me when we were both grounded by a snowstorm at the Cleveland airport, which ends with him deeming me a "fine young man," and encouraging me to serve the people, creating the allusion that Jesus himself had ordained me a public servant.

Politics is the art of promising voters everything they want, then convincing them it is someone else's fault when you can't deliver. The truth is, we lie because voters insist upon it. You won't elect us unless we guarantee the impossible. Balance the budget? Here are your choices. Choose one:

A. Raise taxes.
B. Slash entitlements.
C. Cut the defense budget.

And you choose…none. See the problem?

You only accept facts that support your narrative. You want us to do something about gun violence, but you don't want to give up your guns. You worry about climate change but insist upon drinking from disposable petroleum-based plastic containers while piloting yacht-sized vehicles. You use sparse drinking water to keep golf courses green. You bemoan the high cost of health care while subsisting on a sugar-based diet that leaves you obese and gasping for air. You complain your kids are turning into digital zombies, but instead of having a conversation or reading to them, you plop them in front of an iPad filled with addictive imagery created by Chinese spies while you post online pictures of your fake perfect life.

So, you live a lie, and politicians reciprocate. As my good friend Jack Nicholson once said, "You can't handle the truth."

Remind me to tell you about the time Jack and I rode Harleys across the Southwest.

This is all quite distressing for the ten percent of politicians really trying to accomplish something, but for the failed actors comfortable with fake facts, it is part of the job, which, when queried, is probably why most people prefer salespeople hawking extended car warranties to elected officials.

"Why do it?" I am often asked. "Why debase yourself and be the target of constant hatred and ridicule when, given your credentials, you could have a lucrative career in the private sector?"

There are a few simple answers. When I entered the senate, I had a net worth of approximately $180,000. Today I am worth around eighty mil, give or take. Curiously, I've been able to accumulate this wealth while making about the same salary as a mediocre CPA.

I do anything I want. Last minute craving to see the Super Bowl? Private jets are lined up to transport me to a fully paid visit to a skybox. The world's most exclusive restaurants always have a table for me, and, most of the time, someone mysteriously picks up the check. Kid Rock asked *me* for my autograph! While protestors line up outside the gate to accuse me of every kind of heinous crime against humanity, there are always groups anxious to bestow honors.

Of course, I need to be selective. I had to decline the invitation from an Idaho organization that wanted to name me "White Man of the Year," but mixed among the adoring crazies are legitimate organizations that truly do appreciate my work.

You even have a crush on me. Despite credible corruption claims; an alleged spin on Epstein's yacht; that torturous interview with Lesley Stahl; obvious alcohol issues; my inability to commit to any platform to advance society that might harm me in the polls; and a long list of misstatements offensive to women, minorities, LGBTQ, Californians, four Native American tribes, elderly Jews, and most people under age forty, you recently saw fit to elect me to the highest office in the land. Hello, Mr. President!

And that's where things have gotten complicated: the whole "buck stops here" thing. For instance, I might have been a bit hasty in defunding all vaccine research and disbanding most of the federal health agencies, but Patriots for America made a compelling donation during my campaign, and at their behest, I moved most of the health budget to an initiative that provides heavy armaments to local sheriffs' offices. I could be honest and let the public know a nasty brain-rotting virus that we are completely unprepared for has jumped shores into Miami and Seattle, but that would lead to mass panic and a major dip in my popularity. And I guess one could make the case that we will need better-armed police when the plague spreads, and the civil unrest begins.

I also can't see the upside in commenting on the poisonous algae bloom that will soon hit the gulf shores, as there is really nothing that can be done about it. The briefing last night with my science advisors depressed even me, and it seems foolish to tell the American public that a mass of toxic rotting seaweed the size of Arizona will soon decimate the water surrounding four states, destroy their coastlines, and kill all aquatic life. This would certainly call into question my staunch denial of climate change and unwavering support of the fossil fuel industries, and I'm not prepared for that kind of critique.

Plus, people will already be stressed out as their relatives drop dead from brain rot.

At times like this, I wonder why I even wanted this job! This morning I received a rather dire security report about a terrorist cell equipped with tactical nuclear weapons. I dread the inevitable finger-pointing that will occur if one of our major cities loses six square blocks and several hundred thousand citizens to radioactive haze. Despite the fact that these are homegrown radicals, I would be forced to launch a tit-for-tat nuclear strike in the middle east, and it would pain me to order the death of a million people that have no idea why they are being incinerated. Plus, someone will surely point out that it was me that introduced the bill that defunded the CIA and FBI that might have detected the terrorists and moved the money to Sky Force. But imagine if instead of terrorists, we were battling aliens. Nobody would give me credit for that one.

I'm beginning to think the best option for all is for me to make an elegant exit from public life and leave the bad news to someone more qualified to endure the backlash. My vice president, a loud Southern woman of limited intellect and angry pessimism, seems tailor-made for the task. Accordingly, I think it best I resign for health reasons, with the subtle but unstated suggestion that a rare and painful disease will soon relegate me to the hall of past presidents. Perhaps sarcoidosis of the heart, a little-known but scary-sounding affliction. America will understand and honor my service, and hopefully, the press will respect my decision to pass with privacy.

A former donor has offered to host me at his lovely private island off the coast of Belize, and Sylvia and I will retreat there with her two beautiful French assistants, who will offer solace to both of us. The island paradise will be a safe place to ride out whatever hellish scenarios might befall the world. And who knows? Perhaps in a few years, after the radioactive dust has settled and the pandemic has retreated into the jungle, I might again be of service. The story of my miraculous recovery from a terminal disease will be inspiring to a beaten-down and thinned population anxious to reconnect with a trusted leader. I have concocted quite a tale of how I orchestrated relief efforts from the confines of my bed. Of course, all this assumes there is something left to govern. It's a little soon to tell.

But if the opportunity to serve presents itself, you can depend on me, your devoted public servant.

REUNION

Becca had positioned it on the dining room table as if she were exhibiting a personal note from the Pope; the green envelope propped up against a crystal Mikasa candlestick holder, a yellow sticky attached to the side proclaiming, *LET'S GO TO THIS!* in precise cursive, her signature tiny heart scribbled at the bottom.

Gil grimaced. *Nothing good comes in the mail anymore.* The Postal Service had morphed into the preferred delivery system for the IRS and shady gutter salesmen. The worst letters arrived in fancy padded envelopes. Graduation announcements from a cousin you never liked. Wedding invitations from people so unfamiliar you needed to google their names.

If Becca wanted to attend, it probably emanated from one of the obscure charities she supported. Maybe Kid Biz, which helped poverty-stricken youngsters open Etsy stores. Or Dress Best, a nonprofit that distributed hand-me-down designer clothes to immigrants, leaving Gil to wonder if a destitute Guatemalan woman would wear his wife's ecru linen Ralph Lauren pantsuit to her job at the Amazon warehouse.

But he was even more surprised to see the return name on the envelope: *Billings High Class of 1981*, words that jabbed his solar plexus. He didn't need to be reminded that it had been four decades since he graduated from high school. Acknowledging that fact would signal he was cresting middle age and sliding into elderly decline. A creaky future of deep lines cleaving his face, accompanied by a loss of motor skills and bowel control. He had no desire to be confined to a BarcaLounger, staring glassy-eyed at reruns of *Blue Bloods*.

But there was something more disturbing than a reminder of the passage of time. Seeing *Billings High Class of 1981* in print made him physically queasy, like the vomit-inducing aroma of tequila after a bad drunk.

Gil was not one of those people that took pleasure in reminiscing about his teen years. In fact, he barely remembered Billings High and instead regarded it as a necessary bridge between childhood and the success he began to experience in college. High school memories were hazy recollections of insecurity, rage, and sexual frustration served up with a heaping dose of acne.

"Are we going?" Becca appeared in the doorway, several sips into her 6:00 p.m. chardonnay.

Gil examined the invitation. THE CLASS OF 1981 INVITES YOU TO A TWO-DAY CELEBRATION! TIME TO ROCK OUT AGAIN!

"You want to go to Billings? Breathe air recirculated from the Conoco refinery?" Gil asked.

"Sure. I've always wanted to see Billings. See where you grew up. I bet it's beautiful."

"If your idea of beauty includes oil storage tanks and meth labs," Gil said. "Billings is not the Montana you see on television. It's a bit more industrial. And I think you'd get bored hanging around a bunch of strangers rehashing old times."

"Gil, you're such a mystery man when it comes to your upbringing. I've never seen where you were raised. You hardly ever talk about Billings. In fact, I've never met anyone that knew you before the age of thirty. If I didn't know better, I'd think you were harboring some big secret. Were you a Russian spy sent over here when you were in your twenties?" she joked. "I want to see the house where you grew up. Your high school. The place you had your first job."

"The house I grew up in is gone, replaced by a Burger King. And my first job was at RadioShack, so we might be out of luck."

"C'mon, don't you want to check out the hometown?" Becca cajoled. "Catch up with old friends? What about the guy I have heard you mention? Your best friend growing up?"

"Ritchie," Gil said. At the mention of the name, he was overcome with dread, though he wasn't sure why. "Jesus, I haven't thought about him in years. I never spoke to him after graduation."

"Why?"

Gil shook his head, trying hard to recall, but the last few months of his senior year were blurry, as if they occurred in someone else's life. "I don't know. We were close, but I guess we just lost touch. You grow up."

"Wouldn't it be fun to see him?" Becca said. "I want to meet your first girlfriend. Aren't you curious what Lana looks like now?"

"Dana," Gil corrected. "I heard she has four grown kids. I doubt she'd want to see me, especially if she has fond memories of my long-lost mullet. Besides, the music will be awful. Do you want to spend an entire weekend listening to Foreigner and Van Halen?"

"I love Van Halen," Becca gushed. "Imagine showing off your young hot wife?" She thrust a hip forward. "Make all the jocks that used to torment you a little jealous?"

She was joking, but Gil thought she might have a point. Becca was only forty-five. And unlike Gil, Becca actually looked younger, with the face and figure of a woman in her thirties. It suddenly occurred to him that she was five years old when he graduated, which made him wince.

Still, he'd avoided class reunions. He didn't see the point. There was no family left to visit. He wasn't popular in high school and hadn't maintained a relationship with any of his classmates. He doubted anyone would even remember him.

And returning to Billings made him nauseated. He hadn't been there for twelve years and had only returned then to attend his mother's funeral, going in and out in a day.

"The place has bad juju for me," he said. "I never felt comfortable."

"You lived there a third of your life. I want to see what it's like. I'll take care of all the arrangements. It's on your birthday weekend, so it will be a celebration trip," Becca said. "You can just catch up with old friends and have a ball."

Christ. He would turn fifty-eight at the reunion. Talk about insult to injury.

Arguing was pointless once Becca made a decision. He decided he would bank on the fact that it was months away, and she would forget, or something more important would come along. "Okay." He held up his palms. "I cannot deny you the wonders of the magic city. Refineries, the sugar beet factory, lots of tiny disgusting casinos. We will experience it all."

That night he awoke in a familiar panic, adrenaline surging as he bolted up in bed. He'd hoped the dreams were gone for good, but tonight they'd come roaring back, stronger and more realistic than ever. Trying not to wake Becca, he crept into the kitchen to down a glass of water, clenching his fists as tension vibrated through his body, an erection pushing hard into his underwear.

SEVEN MONTHS LATER, THEY were returning from a Fourth of July party when Becca made it clear the reunion had not slipped her mind. She reached into her purse and produced an agenda. "We leave Friday morning for Billings. It's an easy flight; we'll be there by noon. I rented a car and booked reservations at a hotel called The Northern. It looks really nice."

Gil frowned. "You really want to do this?"

"We are going to your reunion," Becca said firmly, "and I have planned an incredible birthday weekend for you. I got the presidential suite, and it was only $350 a night. The town is a bargain. Friday night we're going to something called Kegger on the Rims. I know what a kegger is, but what are the rims?"

The rims were one of the things Gil hated most about his hometown: jagged, rattlesnake-infested crags lauding over the city. The elite had homes underneath the cliffs, so saying you lived "on the rims" bestowed a kind of social superiority he'd always found disgusting. "Billings is surrounded by a sandstone bluff they call the rims," he explained. "When I was in high school, we would go to a spot on the rims overlooking the city, build a big bonfire out of pallets, and have a kegger. Half the time the cops would show up and shut us down. It was also the place you would go to park and make out with your girlfriend. With all the houses they've built around there, I'm surprised there's still a place to hold a party."

"I love making out," Becca smiled. "Did you and Dana spend a lot of time on the rims?"

"We spent a few evenings parked there."

"Well, maybe we can relive your glory days tonight. I'd be up for a make-out session." She nudged him. "The invitation says the kegger is dedicated to the memory of Danny Westmont. Who's that?"

Gil flushed at the mention of Danny's name. "That was sad. We had a big kegger on graduation night, and Danny got drunk and fell off the rims and died. Broke his neck, and nobody found him until the next day."

"Oh, my God, that's terrible. Did you know him well?"

Gil hesitated. "I wouldn't call us friends, but we went to grade school and junior high together, so I'd always known him. He was odd. I'm pretty sure he was gay, but in those days, you could never admit anything like that. People really tormented him."

"Jesus, kids can be so awful," Becca said. "What did they do?"

"The standard homophobic stuff that used to somehow be okay. Called him names, shoved him around. They were always painting 'fag' on his locker. He had an old Chevy he was proud of, and someone painted a big dick on the door. That kind of thing."

"Disgusting."

"Yeah, it's ironic that some of the people that hassled him will probably be there tonight celebrating his memory."

"Thank God times have changed."

Gil nodded, hoping that was true.

AS GIL HAD PREDICTED, the rims looked a lot different than the last time he had visited. Luxury housing developments with fifty-mile views of the Beartooth Mountains dotted the bluff, and the hiking trails he had enjoyed as a kid were now blacktop and manicured lawns.

But somehow, their old kegger spot had survived the development. They pulled the rental car into a field that held at least thirty vehicles and walked down a trail toward blaring music. Gil was growing increasingly nervous. "Remember, this was your idea," he said to Becca.

She grabbed his hand and smiled. "We're going to have a blast!"

The setting had not changed. A pickup with a keg perched on the tailgate was the center of the party, and people milled around it, filling red plastic cups. Gil thought he recognized several faces, though it felt more like seeing his classmates' grandparents. There was a card table near the pickup, and two women were handing out name tags.

"Gil and Becca Ryan," he said to one of the women.

"Gil, is it really you?" The woman stood up, rushed around the table, and hugged him. "Gil," she said, hands on hips, expressing faux outrage he didn't recognize her, "I'm Debbie Weekly." She turned to Becca. "Your husband and I were on the newspaper staff. We had a lot of good times."

Becca had the gift of instant intimacy, and she hugged Debbie like a long-lost sister. The two engaged in a discussion about sixteen-year-old Gil's hijinks, though he had no recollection of the stories that seemed so clear in Debbie's memory. "I'll get us a couple beers," he said, when the conversation turned to Becca's real estate career.

He felt a painful déjà vu as he approached the keg. Three men stood near it, and he realized that forty years ago, they would have occupied the same position. Wayne Edwards, Vince Thiel, and Dick Fallon were gone-to-seed athletes, their once-fit frames now hunched and damaged, encased in layers of middle-age flab. Still, they loomed over the place.

He threw them a shy "hey" as he filled the cups.

Dick smiled and said, "Gil Ryan?"

Dick had existed in a social stratosphere that Gil assumed to be off-limits and was shocked he knew his name. "Yeah, good to see you, Dick," he replied, offering greetings and handshakes to all three men. They were surprisingly friendly, and it occurred to Gil that he might have misjudged the situation. Perhaps his discomfort about the reunion was based on childish insecurities that he'd never managed to exorcise from his psyche. Time was the great equalizer, and it was ridiculous to feel the same stress he'd suffered as a sixteen-year-old constantly lamenting his lack of social stature.

They had been talking for over ten minutes when Becca rushed toward him and grabbed his hand. "I have a surprise for you," she said, pulling him from the group, which perturbed Gil. He would have been happy to spend the rest of the evening observing the festivities from the cool guy perch. They walked about twenty feet before he understood her enthusiasm. A much older version of his best friend Ritchie stood in front of him, next to a woman he recognized as a classmate, Sharon something. He faintly remembered the two had started dating right before graduation.

"Look who I found." Becca smiled. "They checked in while I was standing there, and I told them I had to find Gil because he was so excited about seeing Ritchie after all these years."

There was no warmth in Ritchie's expression, and it dawned on Gil that his recollection of their friendship might be skewed. His memories with Ritchie went back to grade school, sharing all things monumental to a kid. They'd ridden their matching Schwinn

Sting-Rays together, floated the Yellowstone in tubes, and cowered on Ritchie's couch to watch *Creature Features* on the cable channel from Salt Lake City. The two had gotten drunk for the first time at Joe Hughes's house, stumbling arm-in-arm only to be confronted by Gil's father. But Gil saw no acknowledgment of their history in Ritchie's eyes.

"Ritchie," he said. Their handshake morphed into a requisite stilted man-hug, and they uncomfortably pulled back. The conversation was a standard curriculum vitae, forty years encapsulated into quick snapshots of education, employment, and in Ritchie's case, details about his two grown children. After a few uncomfortable minutes, Ritchie spotted a convenient familiar face, and the two excused themselves.

"Wow, if he's your best friend, I don't want to meet an enemy," Becca quipped.

"So, I wasn't imagining it?"

"No, that guy clearly does not like you. What happened? It's weird to hold a grudge for forty years. What did you do, sleep with his girlfriend?"

"I have no idea," Gil said, suddenly feeling lightheaded.

Debbie Weekly broke the spell, barging in with two other classmates that had worked on the newspaper, and the conversation soon rang with laughter. Twenty minutes later, the dancing started, and Becca dragged Gil to a clearing where big speakers blasted Hall & Oates, Juice Newton, and REO Speedwagon.

A half-hour later, sweaty and red, Gil made his way back to the keg to refill their cups. Ritchie was standing by himself ten feet from the truck and regarded him with a chilly stare. Gil was tempted to ignore him but felt anger welling up.

"Ritchie, I get the feeling I did something wrong where you're concerned, but I really have no idea what it is." Gil stepped toward him. "We used to be best friends, and I would love to know what happened."

"What happened?" Ritchie smirked. "Jesus, Gil, you know what happened. I can't believe you would show up here. You were a sick kid, and you're even a sicker man. I guess I'm just shocked to see you. I've been praying all these years that you died."

"What the hell is your problem?" Gil took a step toward Ritchie, flashing on the two of them as kids. They had tussled a few times, juvenile wrestling matches gone wrong, which always ended with Gil apologizing for going too far, bloodying Ritchie on more than one occasion. Anger had been a consistent theme for much of his life. Gil acknowledged he suffered a rage problem that had plagued him into adulthood, and now he stopped to calm himself, staring down at his fists, trying to level his breathing.

"Are you really going to act like it didn't happen?" Ritchie said.

"What are you talking about?" Gil pleaded.

Ritchie shook his head. "Did you want to return to the scene of the crime? Is that it? Relive it all? Is that your sick fantasy? Okay, let's do it," he barked, and moved forward to put a guiding hand on Gil's arm. Gil jerked back, but for some reason, felt compelled to follow him past a stand of scrub trees, as if he were being pulled. They walked a hundred feet, through pines and thorny bushes, until they could no longer see the partygoers. A white wooden cross, paint peeling from old, rotted wood, DANNY burned into the surface, had been pounded into the ground a few feet from the edge of the cliff, surrounded by remnants of decayed flowers.

"Remember this place?" Ritchie asked. "Remember Danny Westmont? Jesus, the way you used to torment that poor guy. Calling him names, painting FAG on his locker and car. Accusing him of being what you really were. And he still did anything you wanted. What a sick relationship. Probably because he would have done anything to stop you from torturing him."

Gil looked at the cross, his mind barraged with memories that must belong to someone else. Danny in front of him, fondling him, mouth engorging him, Gil drunkenly giving instruction, when he turned to see Ritchie. The shame that mutated to rage, yelling, "Get away from me, you goddamn queer." Kicking hard at Danny, hoping Ritchie would believe Gil was the victim, his foot catching Danny in the cheek, blood flying from his mouth. Another kick, this one connecting square under his jaw, which sent Danny catapulting over the side of the cliff, a moist thud sounding a second later. Gil falling to the ground with a panicked sob, crawling to the jagged edge, looking down into blackness.

"It wasn't…it couldn't have been…me," Gil said, transfixed by the cross.

"You made me a part of it," Ritchie said. "I should have turned you in. Sent you to prison. But I just turned around and left. Made believe that I hadn't seen what happened. And the next day, when they found his body, I said nothing. I was a coward. Now every day of my life, I think about Danny. About what you did to him, and how I did nothing."

Gil was struggling to breathe, wondering if this was real or another of his nightmares. They'd plagued him for years, and he thought he'd finally beaten them, until he'd received the invitation to the reunion. He turned to see his wife standing fifteen feet away, and he prayed she hadn't heard the discussion. He collapsed and rolled into a ball, hugging his knees hard as dust flew up, rocking side-to-side as he moaned, the cross three feet to his left.

Then Becca was looking down on him, and he hoped she was there to sweetly rouse him. He wanted to sit up in their big bed and shake off the horrible images. But she was crying, demanding, "Gil, is it true?"

And he wondered if this time he might not wake.

WHAT ARE THE ODDS?

Aiden analyzed the clogged traffic, realizing this might be an interesting challenge for his math class.

If there are twenty-eight cars at a red light, and the light turns green for thirty seconds every sixty-five seconds, with five seconds of yellow light, and on average, seven cars proceed through every green light, with one additional during the yellow light, how many minutes will it take for all twenty-eight cars to proceed through the light?

Of course, that would be a relatively simple calculation, appropriate for his freshmen and sophomores, but what if Aiden added real-life variables for his juniors and seniors based on his burgeoning angst as honking erupted around him.

If one out of every nine cars coming in the opposite lane turns left, slowing the flow from eight cars to six, how many minutes will it now take?

He was building the equations in his head when his wife interrupted by blurting, "Unbelievable."

"Bad traffic," he commiserated, it becoming obvious that Diana's blood pressure was elevating as their speed declined. Aiden utilized numbers as a stress reduction tool, often crawling inside his head to the comfort of statistics and equations. While nodding off to sleep, he found it relaxing to envision the infinite progression of the Archimedes Constant, a mathematician's version of counting sheep. He took comfort in the fact that numbers were the only thing in life not subject to interpretation. Society disagreed on everything. But numbers were irrefutable.

His wife didn't possess a similar anxiety hack. Instead, Diana garnered strength via anger. Her job as a litigator encouraged a state of perpetual rage that Aiden found annoying but strangely sexy. Diana was the alpha in their relationship—fighting, and almost always winning, all life's normal battles, while releasing Aiden from the painful obligation to confront a frequently abusive infrastructure. Pity the overcharging cable company or internet provider that crossed them, because Diana would make it her life's goal to receive full compensation for their greed, while metaphorically driving a stake through the heart of any customer service agent foolish enough to challenge her. A framed apology letter, sent from the CEO of Home Depot, hung in a premier position next to her law diploma, a trophy scalp won after she sued and brutalized the giant company for selling them a defective barbecue, then compounded the infraction by denying a refund. While he appreciated the outcomes, Aiden tried to avoid the front-row seat to her ire.

"This fucking town," she said, which was loudly interrupted from the backseat by their seven-year-old son Bobby.

"That's a bad word," he protested. "Word jar, word jar."

Diana laughed, calmed by her son. "That's right, Bobby, I'm sorry. When we get home, I will put a dollar in the bad word jar." But they all knew that Diana's potty mouth was integral to her personality, and any sense of de-escalation was fleeting. "Missoula is a parking lot. I remember when you could get across town in ten minutes. Now it could take thirty minutes, maybe even an hour."

The colonization of their small city by Covid migrants was familiar chatter, and Aiden nodded in agreement. Those who had lived here a decade or more lamented the crowds and nonstop building. They worried that the influx of new residents, combined with an invading force of national companies that drove local vendors out of business, would forever alter their cherished community. It had been shocking to see housing prices rise so fast that even the middle class were forced to flee the city limits for more affordable burbs, while out-of-staters with no appreciation of their town's quirky heritage took control. Aiden loved Missoula's progressive past and persona—a hippie enclave surrounded by red-state Montana—and he did not want to see it change.

But like everything, there were mathematical equations to consider. If one were trying to calculate the "happiness quotient" for a Missoula resident, you would certainly have to deduct points for excessive traffic, inflated housing costs, environmental damage, added crime, and loss of local businesses. But there were additions to the formula. Aiden and Diana loved fine dining—especially unusual cuisines—and the added population now supported at least ten great new restaurants. The local symphony was flush with new members and could afford a full-time director. Diana's law firm—and their finances—were flourishing. He loved the new natural food store and its wonderful fresh fish counter. Most of all, as an educator, he was thrilled with the newfound diversity at school.

Five years ago, the only kids of color he taught were Jose Lopez, whose parents were third-generation Missoulians, and Angeline Tulee, whose mother hailed from the Flathead Indian reservation. But now, his classroom was an American cornucopia. His best student was the daughter of a Pakistani who moved to Missoula to run a start-up tech company. The Musa sisters, stunningly beautiful twin girls with the glistening ebony skin of their native Nigeria, were fluent in three languages. There were Chinese, Filipinos, and a brother and sister from Denmark. And the diversity of those who migrated from within the states had also improved the school. They had a rapper from Atlanta, a Sikh from Detroit, and three kids with same-sex parents. The confining old social groups limited to jocks and nerds had been expanded to include LGBTQ, Spanish speakers, and, much to Aiden's delight, a large technically-oriented subset—many students now realizing that they were much more likely to be successful with a background in math and engineering versus moderate athletic achievements. Class discussions were rich with varying perspectives and life experiences that fostered understanding and creativity.

Not everyone welcomed this kind of environment. A vocal right-wing, pro-Christian group of parents were constantly battling change. Aiden had to be very careful to avoid any overt political or social discussions during class time, lest he or the principal be bombarded with angry folks that perceived any opposing thought as an affront to God and their ideology. Clair Hughes, one of the history teachers, had come under fire while teaching a class on the Civil War, several parents objecting to the fact that she rightly identified slavery as the main cause of the conflict.

"We don't want our kids feeling guilty over something that happened a long time ago," one mother exclaimed at a parent-teacher conference.

"So, we can't teach anything that makes kids feel bad about history? How do you suggest we handle the Crusades?" Clair replied dryly. "And World War II? Should I be sensitive to Nazis?"

Between Covid and politics, teaching was now like stepping through a minefield. It was equally possible to upset the liberal parents. Aiden did his best to stay current on pronouns and terminology for different lifestyles but found it difficult to keep up. In his youth, queer was an insulting term, but now it seemed okay. He was still trying to figure out what cisgender meant. He had made the mistake of commenting to a class that he remembered when Bruce Jenner was on the *Wheaties* box, coming under fire from several students for commenting, "What a handsome guy he was."

"That's insulting to Caitlyn," Liz Mannix scolded. "It should be *what a handsome guy she was.*"

The slightest rebuke to a student might bring retribution. He regularly took phone calls from parents upset their children did poorly on a test. "My son studied hard for that exam," one exasperated mother said to him. "How can you give him a failing grade?"

"Because he didn't get the correct answers," Aiden patiently explained.

"Do you know what it will do to his self-image if he doesn't do well?" the mother countered. Aiden was more concerned about his self-image if he was unemployed.

That was another reason Aiden loved math. There was nothing subjective about the right answers, and it was a difficult subject to parse into political camps. He'd never encountered someone so fanatical about algebra that they hated trigonometry. He just wanted to teach without conflict, so he kept his politics to himself.

Unfortunately, that was impossible in his family life. Aiden faced special challenges with his brother Frank, who had never heard a conspiracy theory he didn't deem logical. The brothers had once been close, and Aiden wasn't exactly sure when they had diverged, but it became very clear they had differing world views around the time Obama was elected. Of course, Frank staunchly denied he had any racist tendencies, but he increasingly felt comfortable pointing out that the decline and browning of America coincided.

Even though Aiden knew his brother had committed a large percentage of the serious sins, including violating a few commandments, Frank recently started pontificating about how the country needed to find Jesus to survive.

"Weird position for an atheist to take," Aiden commented.

Aiden suspected that the real explanation for his brother's transition was anger over his own failures as opposed to any political ideology. Frank fancied himself a businessman but had driven both of his entrepreneurial adventures into bankruptcy before settling down to a job operating heavy equipment. Even though he made a good living working for the county, Frank harped about how government was the enemy, visualizing a hazy world of men-in-black circling his house in helicopters, boiling with an inexplicable anger fed by a steady stream of pablum.

Aiden's patience for his brother was especially challenged by his second amendment rants. Both men had been raised around guns and enjoyed hunting. But the thought of possessing firearms designed to enact mass human casualties was an obscenity to Aiden.

The nubbin of glue that held the brothers together was Frank's son Craig. Aiden had always liked the kid, but his interest was enhanced when Craig showed an aptitude and love for numbers. Craig was in Aiden's junior-level math class and exhibited real talent. Sometimes Aiden saw himself in his nephew's eyes. Craig's head slightly rolled back as he visualized rows of numbers, followed by a slight smile as the solution locked in. Aiden knew that feeling. It was like searching your brain for a long-lost song or movie title, letters and fragments of words flashing by, connecting, and building until the answer locked in.

It was because of Craig they were now sitting in traffic. Aiden had not seen his brother in three months after a major blowout at a family dinner. Diana was not shy about her disdain for Frank—she had secretly nicknamed him Evil Gomer—and during one of his Nancy Pelosi tirades, she chose to put him in his place. It was not a fair battle, as if Frank had brought a fingernail clipper to a gunfight. Diana obliterated him to the point that he slunk away, muttering, "Goddamn bitch."

Craig had called Aiden a week earlier to patch up the family squabble, inviting them to a birthday party for Frank. It had been difficult to convince Diana to attend, but he finally played the "Frank's my last living relative since the folks died card," and she agreed, with the caveat, "The minute Evil Gomer starts any racist, sexist, or QAnon shit I am out of there."

They made it through two lights, but at the third, the intersection was blocked by a fender bender. "We're going to be really late," Aiden said to his wife. "Would you mind texting Frank and letting him know?"

"Or I could tell him we can't make it. You know, use the car wreck as an excuse," Diana said sweetly.

"C'mon, you agreed," Aiden said.

"Mom, *why* are we going to Uncle Frank's house? I thought you said you never wanted to see him again." Bobby leaned forward as far as the rear seatbelt allowed. "You said he was a macaroon."

"It's moron, and I did not say that." Diana admonished. "Your dad and I were having a private conversation, and you shouldn't be listening."

"We weren't listening," Audrey, their sixteen-year-old daughter, piped up from the backseat. "You were arguing, and we couldn't avoid hearing. You said Uncle Frank is a racist, sexist, gun-loving moron, and you didn't want to be around him."

"Listen. People—even parents—sometimes say things they don't mean," Aiden said. "Frank is your uncle, and we love him. We might have some political differences, but we're family. I want you kids to have a good relationship with Craig."

"Craig's a freak," Audrey said. "He looks at me and all my friends with those googly psycho eyes, and I heard he had a boner in Mrs. Manley's class."

"Don't be spreading rumors like that," Aiden snapped. "I wish you were as good a student as your cousin."

"What's a boner?" Bobby asked.

Diana laughed and nudged her husband. "I'll let you handle that one."

"Listen, I want everyone to behave this afternoon," Aiden said. "We're all family, and despite our differences, we love each other, so no arguing. Let's just celebrate your uncle's birthday."

He was anxious to change the subject and noticed a group of girls gathered on the corner by the museum. Two were dressed in skin-tight pants that looked like leather or vinyl with skimpy tops that he would never allow his daughter to wear. The shorter of the two was wearing a black and purple wig and knee-high boots that looked like dominatrix garb. The other wore enormous red slated sunglasses that couldn't possibly enhance vision. They were dancing in front of the modernistic steel statue at the entrance to the museum, with moves more sexual than rhythmic. He turned toward Audrey. "Do you know them?"

She rolled down her window, the loud bass beat of a song Aiden didn't recognize vibrating inside the car. "Oh yeah." She nodded. "Online, they call themselves The Slutty Sisters, but they're not really sisters. Their real names are Iris and Allison. I have no idea if they're sluts," she laughed. "Probably. They want to be TikTok stars. That's Cardi B and Bad Bunny."

Aiden only comprehended half of his daughter's words but nodded. He'd noticed over the last few years that the hallways of the high school were being transformed into film sets, students videoing themselves dancing, fighting, flashing body parts, performing cruel pranks, making obscene gestures, and generally doing anything to draw attention online. It felt unhealthy for young minds to be so narcissistic. Or was it insecurity?

When asked what they wanted to do for a living when they graduated, several of his students replied they wanted to be "influencers." *What knowledge did a seventeen-year-old from Missoula, Montana, possess that warranted them being revered across the planet for their wisdom?* He was concerned that teens were willing to go to any length to become celebrities—with no distinction between fame and infamy.

He remembered taking guitar lessons in high school, with a fleeting dream of being the next Eddie Vedder. That seemed a healthier goal than being renowned as the guy who was willing to ram his head full speed into a locker to get Instagram likes. As the traffic cleared and the car began to move, The Slutty Sisters were gyrating and feigning masturbation, Cardi B screaming, "fuckit, fuckit, fuckit."

"Bad word jar," Bobby yelled out the window.

Frank was putting beer in the cooler when the text pinged from Diana, letting him know they would be late. "Here's a big surprise," he said, motioning at his phone. "The Wicked Witch of Missoula says they're running behind. They probably had to stop so she could refuel her broom."

"Oh, Frank, c'mon," his wife Anita said. "You promised to be nice to her."

"That woman is a major part of the problem," he snapped, turning red. "She works for all these big corporations that are coming to Missoula and ruining the town. She spreads all this woke bullshit that has people believing they don't have to work or take responsibility for their own actions or excuses them for acting like perverts. And that superior attitude she has, looking down on us. Someone needs to just stand up to her and—"

"Can't we just all get along for two hours and celebrate your birthday without arguing?" Anita interrupted. "Craig went to a lot of work to put this all together for you."

He looked up and sighed. "Yeah, okay," he said. "Where is Craig? I need his help."

"He's in his room wrapping your present," Anita said. "He was very excited about it, so make sure you act impressed when you open it."

Upstairs Craig stuck the bow on the package, thrilled to anticipate his father's reaction. Even though his mother had helped him pay for it, the gift had been Craig's idea. He had done the research to find just the right model, memorizing the impressive statistics. The *Lasermax LMS* laser sight had a wavelength of 600–700 NM and was accurate within 1.5-inch POI@10 yards. It was designed to factory fit the Glock 43, his dad's favorite pistol, and the go-to gun for his concealed carry permit. The laser sight would really trick it out, and Craig couldn't wait to see it in action. He loved the scenes in movies and video games when the red dot magically appeared on someone's chest, signaling the unseen assassin had found them. *Imagine looking down to see a tiny red circle above your heart.* A 9mm bullet travels at 1,250 feet per second, 852 mph—ninety mph faster than the speed of sound—so by the time you saw the spot, you were technically dead.

Craig heard his dad hollering and inspected himself in the mirror before going downstairs, running a comb through his hair, smoothing his shirt, and lacing up his all-black Nike Ebernons. He'd spent ten minutes contemplating what to wear and finally decided on his Hurley joggers and a Tower Records T-shirt he found at Devine Trash Vintage. He was too young to have ever visited a Tower Records but knew that it was really cool to listen to music on vinyl, and he planned someday to get a turntable and start a record collection. Hopefully, the T-shirt would give him an air of sophistication. Audrey would be with his aunt and uncle, and he wanted to impress.

He knew you weren't supposed to have carnal thoughts about your cousin, but he'd never been able to keep from fantasizing about her. Even when they were young and devoid of any sexual urges, she had spurred something inside him. It was obvious she did not share the emotion, in most situations showing outright disdain, which was painful. Still, he couldn't stop from hoping a switch would flip as they aged, and she'd suddenly view Craig with the same adoration he held for her.

While it was illegal in Montana for first cousins to marry, it was allowed in California, and Craig often daydreamed about moving there with Audrey. In his favorite fantasy, they were both enrolled at UC Santa Barbara. They could rent a little apartment near the beach, while Craig completed his doctorate in mathematics. Audrey would study music or art, their weekends spent wandering the beaches hand-in-hand, skin perpetually warm and tan, Audrey's wardrobe consisting of tiny shorts that accented her long brown legs.

Craig went downstairs to receive instructions from his dad and was outside lighting the barbecue when they arrived. Uncle Aiden yelled a happy greeting and gave him a hug. He glanced around to make sure his father wasn't watching before approaching Aunt Diana—figuring his dad would perceive him as a traitor if he saw them touching. He pushed hard into the embrace, his aunt's large, grown-woman's breasts spreading warmly across his thin chest. Someday Audrey would look like her mom, and probably inherit her curvaceous figure. His dad never liked Diana, and Aiden was often embarrassed and angry at the way she openly ridiculed his father, but he could see Audrey's future in her face, and it made him ache. He gave Bobby a high five and turned toward Audrey, arms extended, ready to move in.

"Don't even think about it," she said, walking past him.

Craig was wounded, but not surprised. She always ignored him at school, too. His dad had warned him about the women in her family. "Stay away from her," he had advised months earlier when he noticed Craig's eyes following her. "She's your cousin, for god's sake. Besides, the women in that family are trouble. Diana thinks her shit don't stink, and she's probably turned her daughter into a major pain in the ass. You know what a cuckold is?"

Craig shook his head.

"It's a man that allows a woman to dominate him. Some sick bastards take pleasure in letting a woman walk all over them. A cuck doesn't even care if their woman has sex with other men; that's how twisted they are. I think Diana's turned my brother into a cuck. He used to be strong, but Diana's done something to him." Frank put an arm around Craig's shoulder and moved closer. "Make sure when you get in a relationship you don't let the female take control. A good woman is strong, but she understands God's order. Men run the show. If you let a woman take over, she'll initially think it's a good thing—a chance to spread her wings a bit—but eventually, she'll end up resenting you. Women love strong men."

As Audrey walked away to greet his mother, Craig wondered if he was the cuckold. Maybe she didn't respect him, didn't understand how powerful he really was. Maybe that was the problem.

~

MUCH TO AIDEN'S RELIEF, the first hour of the gathering went well. They had narrowly avoided a close call when Frank made a joke about the current right-wing insult du jour—masking "fuck Biden" sentiments with a less offensive slogan. Diana had pointed out what a juvenile way that was to express a political opinion, and much to everyone's surprise, Frank agreed.

"I didn't like it when your folks call Trump obscenities, so I guess I have to give Biden the same leeway," he said.

"Thanks, Frank," Diana said, as Bobby pointed out it was also a bad-word-jar offense.

But too much alcohol seldom improves relationships, and Aiden watched warily as both his wife and brother exceeded reasonable limits. Frank was consuming what Aiden calculated as his fifth beer, and he had lost track of how many times Diana had refilled her glass from the pitcher of margaritas. The mood blackened, and now his brother and wife seemed on edge, like boxers circling for the first punch.

Frank jabbed with a derogatory comment about Al Gore. The former Vice President was scheduled to deliver a speech on climate change at the university, which drew condemnation from the right. "That hypocrite is going to fly across the country in his private jet to tell us all how to cut back," Frank said.

"Gore does not travel in a private plane. That's just more propaganda from the idiots you watch on television. And he's been right about climate change from day one." Diana countered. "Jesus, Frank, haven't you noticed what's been going on around here. Montana's on fire the entire summer now, and our rivers are drying up." The subject quickly veered to a comparison of news sources, with voices elevating as words like communist, redneck, snowflake, and fascist were delivered with increasing hostility.

Aiden attempted to intervene, urging both to change the subject, but it had progressed too far. Diana was in her element, with a far superior knowledge of the facts; a trained fighter facing an amateur. This made Frank increasingly angry, throwing out personal insults.

"C'mon, you two," Aiden yelled. "Let's just calm down. Let's change the subject."

CRAIG COULDN'T STAND TO watch his father be ridiculed by his aunt. He moved toward the patio where the food and drinks were set up. Audrey was sitting in a lawn chair looking bored, sipping a lemon mineral water.

"I'm so sick of this," he said.

"Sorry, but your dad's an idiot," she said.

"And your mom's a bitch," he countered. It felt good to stand up to her for once.

"There you go," Audrey said. "Show how sexist you really are. A strong woman is a bitch. Women aren't allowed to have opinions. They should just sit back and listen when morons spout nonsense."

"I'm not sexist," Craig said. "I don't agree with everything my dad says, but your mom takes it too far. People are allowed to have different opinions."

"Facts are facts," Audrey countered dismissively. "You need to get your head out of your ass and read a little bit instead of just listening to Fox News."

Craig glared at his cousin, for the first time considering he might not be in love with her. Maybe his dad was right about the women in her family. He rushed off to the basement, reaching to the top of the door jamb to retrieve the key to the gun safe. He'd fantasized about this moment, but never thought it would really happen. Usually, he visualized storming into school, as the kids that ridiculed or ignored him cowered on the ground weeping. A few weeks earlier, he'd seriously considered showing up at Prom. He'd love to see the faces of all the popular kids—especially the two girls that turned down his invitation—when he came in firing. But this somehow seemed to be the right time.

He swung open the metal door and examined the eight weapons, finally pulling out the ominous-looking AR-15, running numbers in his head. A shotgun would be more efficient at close range, but with a five-shell capacity, he would have to reload, which would take at least thirty crucial seconds. Plus, there was something so much sexier about using an assault rifle. The shooters in the news that used ARs always seemed more impressive. He wished this gun was equipped with a laser sight. He'd love to see Audrey's face when the red dot hit her chest, see the respect she had for him when she realized what was happening.

His head filled with more calculations. His dad had equipped the AR with a larger forty-shell clip. In semiautomatic mode he could probably fire one to two shots per second, so the entire episode would last twenty to thirty seconds. A bullet would travel at 2,000 feet per second, too fast to avoid, and with four targets and forty shells, he would only need 10 percent accuracy, which seemed doable, but he had to consider the stress, and of course, everyone would be running. He'd carefully studied shooters, and in comparison, this did not seem difficult. Adam Lanza killed twenty-six people at Sandy Hook. Nikolas Cruz shot thirty-four people at Parkland.

As he snapped the clip into the weapon, he realized that he was at a point of no return. Within a few minutes, he would be the most famous person on the planet, at least for a day. Most would revile him, but there would be those that understood the importance of what he had done. His father had warned him that there was a civil war coming, and Craig considered the idea that he might be firing the first shot in the conflict. His father would understand. As he mounted the stairs, he smiled, knowing Audrey was about to learn that he was no cuck.

Aiden was standing between Diana and Frank, arms raised in referee stance. "Listen, both of you, just knock it off. I think it's time to go." He had turned to look for Audrey and Bobby when Craig emerged from the kitchen door. At first, he couldn't register what he was seeing; his nephew's arms wrapped around the assault rifle. *He probably just wants to show us the gun.*

As Craig pulled the rifle to his shoulder and moved into a shooting stance, Aiden's stomach dropped. *Is it possible he's going to shoot us?* It didn't make sense. He quickly tried to calculate the odds, a grid flashing in his head with estimated distances. He could rush Craig, approximately thirty feet. He'd most likely be shot, but it might give everyone else time to get away. There was a plastic chair three feet to his right. He could fling it at his nephew, but that would only momentarily distract him and not provide any cover. Audrey was too far to reach, but she saw Craig and was diving backward. He glanced where Bobby stood ten feet away. He could tackle his son to shield his body and maybe pull him to safety. But would that draw fire to his son? Maybe Craig had no intention of shooting Bobby. Frank and Diana were oblivious, still yelling at each other. He could shove both under the picnic table.

Move, move, move, he told himself. *But what should he do? What are the odds?*

THE IMPERSONATOR

MARCOS NUDGED HIS TESLA around two tall panel trucks blocking the circular driveway, barely navigating the slim corridor into the garage between a bright yellow Hyundai he didn't recognize and his wife's Porsche. The caterers had arrived en masse to set up the evening's festivities, and from the size of the army carting tables, cases of wine, massive silver bowls, and plates and utensils into his backyard, Marcos assumed the budget he'd established for the event had been ignored. But he wasn't surprised.

"Do you want the party to be average or out-of-this-world fucking fantastic?" his assistant Christina sarcastically queried in her charming English accent when he'd asked her and his wife to take charge of the affair. Christina had a fascinating way of manipulating language to make any idea she didn't originate sound ridiculous.

"C'mon, Christina, you know Marcos only does fantastic," Marcos' wife, Donna, interjected. "Honey, don't worry, we'll take care of it, and it will be the best fundraiser in the history of fundraisers."

"What's the price difference between average and fantastic?" he'd jokingly asked. "How about just great? I assume great is cheaper than fantastic?" But Marcos knew better than to negotiate. By turning the event over to Christina and Donna, he was assured it would be top-notch, but at a price. He decided to grin and bear it, figuring there were worse investments than raising money to fight Parkinson's disease. And though he didn't like to admit it, he did want to impress the high rollers that would be attending. It might be good for business.

He trailed a troupe of men hauling wooden folding chairs around the side of the house, where he discovered Christina and Donna perched on the elevated ledge of the hot tub, like generals controlling a battle from the bluff. Donna was holding a clipboard with diagrams scribbled across wide sheets of paper. "Tony, the champagne fountain needs to be moved back about six feet," she yelled at a man pushing a dolly balancing a dolphin-shaped contraption.

"Am I imagining things or was there a swimming pool there this morning?" Marcos asked, pointing across the lawn. Sheets of clear flooring covered the water.

"People won't be swimming tonight," Donna said, "This is an elegant soirée, not a party at Hugh Hefner's. They'll want to dance. We'll turn on the pool lights, and the entire floor will glow a soft blue. It will be beautiful."

"And I assume that's the bandstand?" Marcos said, motioning to a large platform that had been installed at the back of the lot, where men on ladders were stringing floodlights. "Because we certainly couldn't just have a DJ, even though people love DJs," he said.

Christina leaned in, grabbed his arm, and whispered into his ear. "Not a band, darling. An orchestra. A big one too. Twelve pieces. With a singer who sounds just like Diana Krall. Hell, for what you're paying, it bloody well should be Diana Krall."

"Wonderful," Marcos said. "Is the bar open yet? Because I should begin drinking."

"No, you have work to do before the cocktail hour. One of your impersonators has arrived. You need to brief all of them on what you want them to do tonight," Donna said. "You'll really get a kick out of this guy. I stuck him in the den."

It had been Marcos' idea to sprinkle a few celebrity impersonators throughout the crowd. A year earlier, they'd attended a function that featured a couple doing hilarious Sean Connery and Dolly Parton impressions, and it had been the hit of the evening. He'd hired three for tonight and planned to download funny details to each of them about the guests they would roast.

"Great, is De Niro here?"

"Nope, this guy is certainly not De Niro," Christina said.

WHEN MARCOS WALKED INTO his den, the man was standing near the window, holding a small Plexiglas display case to the light with both hands, examining the antique pistol inside.

"It's a Spanish Miquelet," Marcos said. "Circa 1780. Very rare. Are you interested in antique firearms?"

Startled, the man put the case down. "Firearms? Oh, guns." He smiled. "Yeah, I love guns. Absolutely adore them. Nobody loves guns more than me. Used to own a lot of them. I kept an Uzi in the closet in my office. A gift from Bibi. Years ago, I was sailing on Putin's yacht, and we shot a Beluga whale with a fifty-caliber sniper rifle from a quarter mile away. Unbelievable." The man moved closer and lowered his voice. "One time, on the way to dinner, I was showing Regis Philbin the derringer I kept under the seat and accidentally blew the back window out of the limo. Scared the shit out of us. The driver thought we were drawing sniper fire." He chuckled. "I even tried to buy a tank. Thought it would be an interesting attraction at one of my golf courses. But of course, county regulators put the kibosh on that one. Hard to get anything done with all this government regulation." He shook his head sadly. "Nobody fought that more than I did."

Marcos laughed out loud. What an act! He could tell this guy was going to liven up the party. "Yeah, what kind of commie government doesn't allow a guy to own a tank," he joked. "Thanks for coming," he said, walking toward the man and raising an arm to shake hands. "I'm Marcos Gallardo."

The man blanched at the site of the palm, as if being forced to touch infected meat, and slowly raised his own to deliver a quick, weak grasp. "Yeah, nice to meet you. Donald Trump."

"That's great," Marcos laughed. "I guess you guys stay in character the entire time?"

The man gave Marcos a quizzical look. "Wadda ya mean, stay in character?"

Marcos nodded, happy to go along with the act. "Okay. Glad to have you here, Mr. Trump. I'm a big fan."

"Gallardo?" The man said, nodding his head in thought. "Italian?"

"Actually, Mexican," Marcos held up his arms in mock surrender. "My parents immigrated when I was three. Please don't deport me."

The man looked confused. "Wha…? Oh, the Mexican stuff. Yeah, that was overblown. Fake news. I actually love the Mexicans, and they love me. Just not the murderers and rapists, but who'd want those kinds of guys for friends? Am I right? The fake press got it wrong, as usual." He scanned the room. "So you work here, or…" He shook his head, waiting for Marcos to finish the thought.

"No, I don't work here." Marcos thought he might be taking the act a bit too far. "I own the place. I hired you."

"Oh," the man perked up. "Good for you. See what I mean? You're one of the good ones. Ever heard of Carlos Slim? One of the richest guys in the world. Mexican. He's a very close friend of mine. Carlos loves me. We need more of your kind in this country. That was always my point. You want America to be great again? Just fill it with great people. Makes sense." He moved toward the window. "Lovely place," he said, waving at the backyard. "Looks like you're going to have a hell of a party. Glad to help. Is that your wife?" He motioned at a heavyset Hispanic woman in a white uniform helping stock the bar. She was at least twenty-five years older than Marcos.

Marcos frowned, then decided to just roll with the gag. "No, *that's* my wife," he said, pointing at Donna.

"Wowee," the man said admiringly. "Look at her. Nice. You and I have similar taste in women. All legs and ass. I like that. She could be a model, and believe me, nobody knows models like I do. The models love me. What nationality?"

Marcos smiled. This guy was playing Trump to the hilt. "American. She was raised in Santa Barbara, two hours from here."

"Really?" The man sounded surprised. "I would've guessed she was an import. She reminds me of Ivana when she was young. In any case, congrats, a really nice piece of ass." He cocked his head to look at Marcos. "Course, I bet you've had your share, a good-looking guy like you. You know, you resemble a friend of mine, Scott Baio. Remember him? He's Italian, probably why I thought you were too. But I think he played a Mexican. Chachi? That's Mexican, right? Italians and Mexicans. Both are swarthy. Easy to mix-up. Another friend of mine, Antonio Sabàto, he's Italian, but a lot of people think he's Mexican. I used to say, 'Hey, Antonio, go clean my pool.' You know, as a joke. He thought it was hilarious. Italians love me too. I used to tear it up with those guys. We'd go out on the town. They tended to draw the young bimbo types. The more sophisticated women, models and such, they'd be all over me. What a team we made. A three-man pussy patrol."

Marcos couldn't decide whether this guy was the world's greatest actor or a complete moron, but he had to admit his resemblance to Trump was uncanny. He was the same height, albeit with the stoop of a man in his mid-eighties. He wore his stringy hair in a thin bouffant, dyed the trademark pumpkin orange that somehow extended to his complexion. The suit, though threadbare and tight around the arms, was his standard dark blue with a red tie. If Marcos didn't know better, he would've guessed this man was the former president.

Nobody had really seen the Donald since his meltdown five years earlier after losing the second election in a landslide. The consensus was that he'd suffered a nervous breakdown, played out in his infamous rant for a few billion people to witness. Trump standing on the stage screaming, "Let the revolution begin, patriots. Storm the White House!" before falling to the floor and rolling into a fetal position.

Photos circulated a year later when he was forced into bankruptcy and sent to prison for eight months. The repossessed properties rebranded, Trump Hotels now sported Hyatt logos, and the golf courses were named for the new owner, Michael Bloomberg. Rosie O'Donnell had purchased the rights to the Trump brand for three thousand dollars at a bankruptcy auction and symbolically retired it by burning Trump clothing, diplomas, and menus from his restaurants in a bonfire held in Rockefeller Square and broadcast live on *The Tonight Show*.

But the public's attention span was as fickle as a cat chasing a ball of yarn. Since he'd been released, Trump had been erased from the public eye, his name morphed into a curious historic relic—the Members Only jacket of politics. Every now and then, he would be featured on sleazy "where are they now" banner ads, his face plastered between elderly cast members of *The Brady Bunch* and photos of Steven Seagal.

The man was examining photos covering a wall. "Beautiful family you have. Nothing more important than family. I hope to patch things up with my kids. I missed seeing Barron grow up, but after the divorce, things were tough. Especially after Melania married that actor." The man bowed his head in sadness. "You know, Barron's in his twenties now and doing great. He did really well in college, top of his class. Well, DeVry. I guess that's a college. Studied iPad repair. I think that's a tremendous field. But it's tough. People like to blame me for everything that goes wrong. When the oldest boys had to go out and get jobs, it somehow became my fault. But you know, I hear Don Jr.'s doing fantastic. Enterprise Car Rental is a wonderful company. Families have disagreements. It will all turn out."

He brightened up and pointed at diplomas behind the desk. "Well, well. Undergrad at UCLA, MBA from Stanford. Impressive. Those are pretty good schools. I'm a Wharton guy. Top of my class. Some people call Stanford the Wharton of the West Coast. You should be proud."

Marcos decided he'd had enough of the Trump shtick. "Okay," he said, motioning at a chair for the man to sit down. "Let's discuss the guests. I want to highlight a few of the big givers, provide a little background, and when they get here, I'll point them out, and you can kid them a bit. Pay extra attention to them. Maybe act like you know them. That might be funny." He pulled out several sheets of paper. "Our biggest donors are Allen and Beverly Lewin."

The man held up a hand in excitement. "Lewin? Jewish? Cause I gotta tell you, despite what you might have heard, I do great with the Jews. Don't believe any of the fake press. My daughter is technically part Palestine Indian. Married a Jew. You want to raise more Hebrew dough, I'm your guy."

Marcos wondered if this was a good idea. The man was beginning to seem unhinged. "Actually, I don't think this crowd will find any of the racist bits funny, and don't worry about trying to raise money. I'll take care of that. Just go up to them, maybe say something like, 'Hey, Allen and Beverly, I haven't seen you in years. How's the dental supply business?' That kind of thing. You know, just get a laugh. Tell a few of the people that they're fired. Harmless stuff, nothing too political."

The man looked baffled. "Racist?" He thought a second, then leaned in as if a light bulb had illuminated in his carroty head. "Okay, I see where you're going, but let me give you a better idea. What if I told you I could double whatever you planned to raise tonight? As I'm sure you've heard, I'm an absolutely fantastic salesman. I literally wrote the book on it. People say I'm the best that ever lived, and I'm confident I could get your guests to give more."

Marcos nodded politely, anxious to move on. "Sure, that would be nice. But we've really got this handled…"

The man held up a hand to interrupt. "Think of it. I help you raise an additional million dollars, and my commission is only twenty percent."

"No thanks," Marcos said firmly. "I just want you to entertain people for a couple hours. Please, no fundraising, and we certainly don't pay commissions on donations. That would be unethical."

The man held up his hands in surrender. "Understood. Just trying to help. What about ten percent? Since it's for charity, I'd be willing to do that. A good cause and all."

They turned when Christina gave a soft knock at the door and peeked in. "Marcos, just wanted to let you know that Robert De Niro and Lady Gaga are waiting in the living room, and you also need to get dressed, as the guests will start arriving in less than an hour."

"Bobby's here?" the man said excitedly. "We go way back. New York and all. But I'm not a fan. He's totally overrated. What an asshole."

"Just your fellow impersonators," Marcos said impatiently. "Listen, read through these guest bios, and Christina or I will point them out at the party. Make them laugh. That's all you need to do."

The man took the sheets. "Got it. Uh, if you don't mind, we might as well get the fee out of the way, so you don't have to worry about it later tonight."

"Christina handles that. She'll pay you."

"Good enough." The man smiled. "This is going to be a tremendous night. Really tremendous. The best night you've ever had. Trust me."

THREE HOURS LATER, MARCOS had to agree that it was shaping up to be a magical event. Donna and Christina had outdone themselves. The backyard had been transformed into an outdoor Parisian nightclub. And from all the input he was receiving, the impersonators were also a big hit.

The woman playing Lady Gaga not only looked the part but mounted the stage with the orchestra to perform a very passable version of "Poker Face."

The Robert De Niro impersonator, primarily channeling the actor from his *Goodfellas* period, added an edgy patina to the slightly conservative crowd. One of Marcos' biggest clients excitedly grabbed him while he was standing at the bar. "De Niro was fabulous. I was talking to a friend of mine when he came up to me, looking pretty scary, and saying, 'You talkin' to me? You talkin' to me?' It was great."

Even Trump's gruff persona seemed to be playing well with the crowd. Lowell Baker, the African American Chief of Oncology at UCLA Medical Center, had patted Marcos on the back while laughing. "The Trump guy is hilarious. He introduced himself, and when I told him what I do for a living, he said, 'That's wonderful. You're a credit to your race. You're the kind of black guy I love.' He looks and talks just like Trump."

Marcos decided he could relax and enjoy the remainder of the night. By his third trip to the martini bar, he was in a better place, his trepidation floating away in a sea of goodwill and Stolichnaya vodka.

Then Christina, looking uncharacteristically frazzled, grabbed his arm and pulled him to a corner of the lawn. "Have you seen Trump anywhere?"

Marcos scanned the lawn but saw no sign of the man. "Not for about a half hour or so. Last I saw, he was talking to a group near the dessert table. He was cracking them up."

"Well, I can't find him," Christina said angrily, "and Marcos, I think I might have really screwed up."

Marcos couldn't recall ever hearing Christina admit to a mistake. "Why? What's wrong?"

"I was in a rush at the beginning of the night, and he asked me to pay him in cash. He told me he would collect for the entire group and take care of it for me."

"Cash? Why cash? Didn't you book him through a service?"

"No," Christina said. "I found him on Craigslist, and I agreed to cash. I don't even know his real name. He lined up the other people. Said he had contacts, so I assumed he knew them. Told me they'd worked together. But De Niro and Lady Gaga are ready to leave now and asked for their money. They told me he found them on a Craigslist ad, and they'd never met him before tonight. He didn't pay them. I think he took off with all the money. Three thousand dollars."

"Jesus," Marcos said disgustedly. "Okay, well, we need to pay them, and then we can figure out what to do tomorrow. We'll call the police."

"Marcos, it gets worse. Allen Lewin pulled me aside and thanked me for the party. He said he had such a good time that when Trump hit him up for an additional donation, he agreed to give another ten thousand. He gave Trump his credit card to go inside and ring it up. That was an hour ago, and he asked me to get his credit card back, because he's ready to leave. Then a couple other guests told me the same thing. I think the Trump impersonator took off with several of the guest's credit cards."

"What?" Marcos began to shout, then quickly lowered his voice. "What are you talking about? You mean…"

He was interrupted by Donna wrapping an arm around his waist. "Nice party, you two. The best we've ever had. Hey, have you seen Trump? The Standleys are ready to leave, and apparently, he took their credit card for a donation. I didn't know you guys had the impersonators raising money too. That's brilliant."

Marcos gave Christina a panicked look. "Check everywhere. I'll look in the house. Go talk to the valets and see if they saw him."

He rushed from room to room, finally ending up in the den, where he sensed something was wrong. Examining the credenza, he realized the antique pistol was gone. He frantically scanned the rest of the room for missing items, and that was when he saw the picture. An eight-by-ten photo had been inserted into one of the gold frames on the wall, covering a family photo taken a year earlier at the beach. Donald Trump, standing in front of a podium, wearing a red *Make America Great Again* cap stared back at him. It was signed:

TO MARCOS, ONE OF THE GOOD ONES. THANKS FOR A GREAT PARTY. DONALD J. TRUMP.

www.ingramcontent.com/pod-product-compliance
Lightning Source LLC
LaVergne TN
LVHW040846180326
834161LV00001B/44
* 9 7 8 1 6 4 4 2 8 5 0 5 3 *